The Greatest
SHOW of All

The Greatest SHOW of All

Jane Eagland

Barrington Stoke

For Selina Pratt

First published in 2016 in Great Britain by
Barrington Stoke Ltd
18 Walker Street, Edinburgh, EH3 7LP

www.barringtonstoke.co.uk

Text © 2016 Jane Eagland

A CIP catalogue record for this book is available from the British Library upon request

ISBN: 978-1-78112-573-1

Printed in China by Leo

Contents

Chapter 1
This house is dark

Kitty opened the back door and listened. From the coach house across the yard she could hear water sloshing in a bucket and the swish-swish of the broom.

Good. That meant Pa was still cleaning the carriages.

Kitty took her chance and nipped into the stable. Inside she took a deep breath – there was nothing in the world as good as that blend of sweet hay and the warm smell of horses. And where else would she want to be today but here, the place where she felt closest to Tom? She went into Shadow's stall and scratched him behind his ears.

"Where is he, Shadow?" Kitty whispered as the dapple-grey horse nuzzled at her. "Do you know?"

She buried her face in Shadow's neck to block out the memory of that dreadful morning exactly a year ago, when she had come downstairs and found the note on the kitchen table.

I'm sorry. I can't be what you want me to be. That's why I'm leaving. Please don't try to come after me.

Tom

Ma had wept and Pa had stormed and raged and then he fell into the black pit of silence he'd been buried in ever since. As for Kitty, she'd tried not to cry, to stay calm for Ma's sake – but the pain was like a hot poker searing her heart. How could Tom have done this? How could he have run away without a word to her before he left?

The note had been the last they'd ever heard from Tom. Pa had made enquiries everywhere he could, but they could find no trace of him.

Kitty sighed. She still loved her big brother despite the pain he'd caused – without him, life was flat and dreary and sad.

Kitty patted Shadow one last time, then stirred herself into action and led the horses out into the yard one by one. She left the bay horse till last and she approached him with wary steps. His name was Demon and, as Pa had said, it suited him – the minute he arrived he'd kicked out and tried to nip Pa's hand. It was a good job he was only staying with them for two nights.

Kitty murmured soothing words to Demon until he was calm enough to move, but she was glad when he was tied up safe, away from the other horses. It would be easy for Pa to clean the stalls now. For once he might even be pleased with her.

Kitty was washing her hands at the tap outside when she heard a noise in the distance. She recognised it at once – the blare of a brass band. It could mean only one thing …

Kitty glanced at the coach house – Pa was still in there. Did she dare?

The music tugged at her and she couldn't resist it. She dashed across the yard and the next moment she was out in the street.

❧❧❧❧

Crowds were lining the High Street, but Kitty managed to wriggle through the crush to the front.

The circus parade was just coming past.

Out in front two clowns in comical wigs and stripy costumes skipped along holding up a broad banner with "HUXLEY'S CIRCUS" painted on it in bold red letters. The brass band marched behind them making a cheerful racket with their trumpets and drums and horns. Then came a stream of acrobats, jugglers and trapeze artists, followed by the ringmaster himself in his scarlet coat.

A tawny lion snarled at the crowd as its cage went by, and behind it two elephants plodded along, their red and gold saddle cloths bright against the grey wrinkles of their skin.

Kitty loved every minute of the parade, but as the last performers approached she pressed her hands over her heart and held her breath. At last, here they were – the horses, trotting by with their heads held high and coats gleaming in the sunshine. As each rider passed by, Kitty studied his face. None of them was Tom.

Kitty dropped her hands and let out her breath. She had hoped – oh, how she had hoped – to see Tom riding past.

Kitty and Tom had only been to the circus once, when they were very small, but they'd never forgotten the magic of it. Ever since then Tom had dreamed of being a circus rider – of riding out into the ring to do amazing tricks on his own horse. He'd practised in secret whenever he could, balancing on his hands on Shadow's back while Kitty held the horse still below him.

Kitty admired Tom's skill and ambition, but she felt sorry for him too. She knew all his dreams would come to nothing and all his effort would be wasted. Pa had made it clear – Tom was to run the stables one day and Pa wouldn't hear of anything else. Tom was his only son – it was his duty to take over the family business.

When Tom disappeared, Kitty was sure that he'd run off to follow his dreams. Whenever the circus came to town, she sneaked out of the stables in the hope of finding him, but she'd always been disappointed. And now she was disappointed all over again.

❀❁❀

When at last the circus was out of sight, Kitty turned and raced home before Pa could notice she was gone. He'd be angry if he knew she hadn't been helping Ma with the housework.

It wasn't just Tom who'd suffered from Pa's stubborn ideas about how things should be done – he had fixed ideas about the tasks it was proper for a girl to take on. But ever since Kitty was a little girl, not even as high as the horses' knees, she'd loved to be in the stable watching Tom and Pa work.

Then, as soon as she was big enough, Tom would let her help with the daily tasks whenever Pa was out – mucking out, grooming and feeding the horses. After a while Tom taught her to ride and then she watched him and Pa like a hawk until she learned how to manage the horses. Soon she could calm them when they were out of sorts and win them round if they were bad-tempered.

Kitty loved it. All of it. Tom had his secret dream and she had hers – to work with horses. When Tom left, upset as she was, it lit a flame of hope in her.

Kitty had gone to Pa and offered to take Tom's place in the stables. But Pa had shaken his head. "Don't be daft, lass," he said. "This is no work for a girl."

At those words, the flame inside Kitty died.

As she reached the gate to the stable yard, Kitty sighed. Then she pushed open the gate, and froze.

Pa was roaring at the bay horse, Demon, and slashing at him with his whip. The horse was rearing, and Kitty could see the whites of his eyes. She couldn't take it in at first – Pa was normally so soft with the horses. She'd never seen him lose his temper with them before.

"Pa, don't!" she cried, and she ran over to him. "Stop! Please stop!"

His eyes blazed as he turned on her. "This is your doing, isn't it?" he shouted.

Kitty stepped back. "What do you mean?"

"You put this devil of a horse out here," her father said. "And when I tried to get him back in, he kicked me. Now I can't get him to budge."

"I'm sorry, Pa." Kitty felt wretched. "Shall *I* try to take him in? He let me bring him out."

"You?" he shouted in her face. "After you've caused all this trouble?" And then he raised his arm.

Kitty gasped and shrank back.

Pa let his arm fall and then, to Kitty's horror, he covered his face with his hands and started to sob.

"Tom, oh Tom," he cried. "Why did you leave us?" Then he lifted his head and gave Kitty a look of disappointment that cut her like a knife. "Why wasn't it you?" he howled. "Why didn't I lose you instead of my boy?"

Chapter 2
Fly away

Kitty fled to her room in the attic, with Pa's cruel words ringing in her ears.

In all her pain and confusion, one thing was clear – Pa hated her. He wanted her gone. So she would have to go. But where? Who would take her in?

Then it came to her – the circus. She could look after their horses and when the circus moved on she would go with it and disappear like Tom. That was what Pa wanted, wasn't it?

And then her heart leaped as she thought that perhaps Tom *was* working at Huxley's, but as a stable hand, not one of the performers. That could explain why he wasn't in the parade.

The idea fired Kitty up with hope, and she began stuffing things into a bag. But then an awful thought struck her. What if the circus owner was like Pa? What if he thought girls couldn't look after horses?

She sank onto her bed in despair. There was nothing for it. She would just have to stay here and face Pa. But his words still tore at her heart.

"My boy ..."

"My boy ..."

All of a sudden, Kitty sat bolt upright. She had her answer.

❧❧❧

Half an hour later, Kitty tiptoed down the stairs feeling very strange indeed.

Her long skirts and bodice were gone and in their place she was wearing a set of Tom's old clothes – trousers, a shirt and a jacket. She'd chopped off her long dark hair with the kitchen scissors and hidden it under her mattress. What was left was a bit ragged but she stuffed it under a cap of Tom's and decided it would do.

She peeped out of the back door. No sign of Pa in the yard.

In a flash Kitty was out of the gate and running down the street. As she raced round the corner, she almost knocked a man down.

"Oi!" he shouted after her. "Watch where you're going, lad."

Kitty grinned in delight. Her disguise was working.

❧❧❧

Kitty reached the market place and stopped. The big top of the circus was already set up in the middle of the square, with the travelling wagons in a neat line along one side. Smoke rose from the chimneys, but there was no one to be seen.

Kitty's heart was beating fast, and not just from running.

What if Tom wasn't here?

Fear swept over her as the reality of what she was about to do sank in. She was going to leave home, leave behind everything she knew. Face the world alone. That was the most terrifying thing. Up till now, she'd always had Ma.

And Pa.

At the thought of Pa, Kitty gritted her teeth. She took a deep breath and strode round the back of the big top where she found more wagons and a huddle of tents. And then she smelled a familiar smell, of straw and animals. She peeped inside the nearest tent – a stables!

Kitty ducked inside and walked along looking at the horses in their stalls. She was careful not to get too close in case she alarmed them. One horse was even lovelier than the others – a beautiful black mare whose stall had a board with 'Opal' chalked on it.

"Opal," Kitty whispered.

At the sound of her name the horse turned her head and flicked her ears. The name suited her. Her dark coat shone with such a blue sheen, she *was* like a lovely jewel.

As Kitty gazed at her, a jingling noise outside made her jump. She tore herself away from Opal and went out of the back of the tent, where she found the two elephants. She was glad to see that each one had a foot tethered by a chain to a sturdy peg in the ground.

The lion was lying in his cage, looking sleepy. But as soon as he saw Kitty, he sprang up and padded over to the bars. Kitty was drawn to him despite her fear, and she took a step forward.

"Careful! Old Nero could rip your arm off!"

Kitty spun round, startled. A boy was standing in the open flap of the stable tent, scowling at her.

"You're not supposed to be here," he said. "We're not open yet."

"I – I haven't come to see the circus," Kitty said. "I'm looking for my brother, Tom Eastwood. Does he work here? At Huxley's."

The boy shook his head. "There's no one called Tom here."

Kitty's heart sank. But the memory of Pa's words and that awful look he'd given her made her rush on before she could change her mind.

"I'm looking for a job," she said. "I'm good with horses, used to stable work."

"Runaway, are you?" the boy said.

"How do you know?" Kitty asked, stunned.

"Oh, we often get lads wanting to join the circus. They think it's all bright lights and excitement." The boy spat on the ground, to show exactly what he thought of runaways.

"I'm not interested in bright lights," Kitty said. "It's the horses I like, looking after them."

The boy's face changed. He put his head on one side and looked at her again. "Can you ride?" he asked.

Kitty nodded.

"All right. Let's see what you can do."

❀❀❀

Ten minutes later Kitty sat astride a tall chestnut mare named Ginger. The boy had warned her that Ginger could be a handful, but as they moved into a trot and then a canter, Kitty felt calm and in control.

When she came to a stop, she was surprised to see a man standing beside the boy. His face was familiar, but Kitty couldn't place him.

As Kitty slid to the ground, the man gave her a shrewd look that made her feel nervous. He had the air of someone who was used to people obeying him.

"So who's this, then, Fred?" he asked.

The boy looked at Kitty.

"I'm Kitt –" Kitty stopped dead and her spine prickled with alarm. She'd given herself away!

"Well, Kit," the man said. "My nephew, Fred here, tells me you want to join us?"

Kitty nodded, almost laughing with relief.

"As it happens, we're a stable lad short," the man went on. "I had to sack the last one for pinching the animals' fodder." He shot another keen look at Kitty. "You won't be trying any of those tricks, will you?"

"No!" Kitty said. Then it sank in that he was giving her a job. "No, sir!" she gabbled. "Thank you, thank you so much. I'll work so hard for you, I'll –"

The man cut her off. "We'll try you out for a week or two," he said. "See how you get on. Fred will sort you out. Got any questions, you ask him."

He winked at Fred and Kitty saw that he had a kind side, under his stern manner.

"I suppose you'll want to watch the show tonight," he said then, with a twinkle.

"Yes, please!"

"Fred will get you in. But have a look round first and get your bearings."

Kitty watched him stride away. "Who is he?" she asked Fred. "I mean, apart from your uncle?"

"Uncle Henry's the guvnor," Fred said.

Kitty gaped at him. "That was Mr Huxley? You mean, your uncle owns the circus – he's the ringmaster from the parade!"

Fred's eyes crinkled as he smiled. "How else could he give you a job just like that? Come on, I'll show you round."

Kitty's heart hammered with excitement as she followed Fred into the stable tent. Whatever she'd wished for herself, she'd never imagined this. If only Tom were here, everything would be perfect.

Chapter 3
A fair young man

Fred showed Kitty where she would sleep and eat and introduced her to the other stable lads.

He didn't say a lot, but Kitty warmed to him. He had a kind manner and, even though he was younger than her, he had a quiet confidence that was appealing. And he hadn't asked any nosy questions, like why she'd run away.

He was showing her where they kept the tools for mucking out, when they heard the band strike up. "Come on," Fred said. "The show's starting."

❧❧❧

It was just as Kitty remembered it – the smell of canvas and sawdust, the way everything gleamed under the lights. The voice of the ringmaster boomed as he introduced amazing act after amazing act to the crowd.

"I now present Pablo the Fearless," he announced, "and, straight from the wilds of Africa, the mighty Nero!"

The lion clawed at Pablo and roared, tossing his magnificent mane and showing his terrifying sharp teeth. Kitty didn't want to watch, but she couldn't tear her eyes away. It was a relief when the lion-tamer took his bow and the acrobats sprang into the ring. Kitty loved the way they threw themselves about as if they had no bones in their extraordinary, elastic bodies.

Then it was the clowns. They made Kitty laugh, tripping over their own feet, sitting on chairs that collapsed and throwing buckets of water over each other. Their leader was a big, beefy clown, and he followed Mr Huxley round and mimicked every move the ringmaster made. The crowd roared with laughter, but Kitty didn't find him funny. He had mean eyes under bushy brows and he bullied the others in a way that seemed wrong to her.

In the end Kitty was glad when the clowns tumbled out of the ring and Sara Fanelli, the tightrope walker, ran in. When she started to dance along her rope, a hush fell over the crowd. Kitty held her breath, entranced. With her hair like fine-spun gold and her costume of sparkling white, Sara seemed to be an angel floating above their heads. Applause like thunder rang out at the end of her act, and then the liberty horses came into the ring.

They were astonishing. They criss-crossed the ring in perfect time, stood up on their back legs to walk and they even danced, swaying together to the music. Kitty clapped until her hands hurt.

But the horse she really wanted to see was Opal, already her favourite.

At last the gleaming black mare galloped in, looking even more like a jewel under the lights. At the sight of her rider, dressed in tight black trousers and a loose-fitting white shirt, Kitty gasped. He had her brother's dark hair and slim build and he rode with the same easy grace.

Could it be Tom riding under a false name?

But as he cantered nearer, she saw that it wasn't him. Kitty could have wept with disappointment. But the boy was so talented and fearless that she was soon caught up in the wonder of his act.

Opal thundered round the ring while he stood up and balanced on one leg and then he jumped over a rope held by two clowns. He sprang up and twisted round so he was facing Opal's tail, then he flipped round to face the front. At the climax of his act, he threw himself into the air, flicked his body over and landed on his feet on Opal's back.

He and Opal left the ring to deafening applause.

And the show was over.

Kitty stayed in her seat until the tent was nearly empty, still in a daze. At last she made her way outside and was enjoying the cool night air, when she heard a voice she knew. Her heart raced as she shrank back into the shadows and peered round. There he was, over by the ticket booth.

Pa!

He was talking to Fred.

Kitty turned and fled. She raced into the stable tent and ducked into Opal's stall. She should be safe here, unless Fred had guessed the truth about her. In which case, he could be telling Pa where to find her right now ... Kitty shut her eyes, as if somehow that would make her invisible.

"All right, Kit?"

At the sound of Fred's voice Kitty snapped her eyes open. He was alone. She let out her breath and snatched a sponge out of a bucket, as if she'd just been cooling Opal off.

"You all right to finish her while I do Ginger?" Fred said.

Kitty nodded. She was still feeling shaky and didn't trust herself to speak.

Fred's voice floated over the barrier. "I got held up by a chap who was looking for his daughter."

Kitty stiffened. "Oh?"

"I told him I haven't seen her."

21

Kitty pressed her face against Opal's flank. She was safe – at least for now.

✿❧❧✿

After all that had happened, Kitty was glad to get to bed in the tent where the stable lads slept. Around her the others snored and muttered in their sleep, but she stayed awake for a long time while the day's events whirled round her mind.

At last she slept, but all night a dark-haired boy on a beautiful black horse galloped through her dreams.

✿❧❧✿

The next day Kitty was putting a bridle on Ginger when she heard a voice call, "Morning, Fred! How's Opal today?"

"She's in good shape, Jack. Eager to go."

Kitty peeped over the barrier to see who it was and her cheeks went hot.

It was him – the brilliant rider she'd seen the night before. He was leaning on a tent pole waiting for Fred to finish grooming Opal.

Kitty took a deep breath, then led Ginger out of her stall.

"Hello!" Jack said. "And who's this then?"

"I'm Kit, the new stable boy." Kitty could hear the wobble in her voice.

But Jack didn't seem to notice. "Pleased to meet you, Kit. I'm Jack."

Kitty wanted to say, *Yes I know and I think your act is wonderful ... I think you are wonderful.* But of course she didn't say any of that, but just stood there, feeling stupid.

Ginger saved her with her fidgeting. "Better go," Kitty muttered. "She needs exercise."

As Kitty walked Ginger round the ring, she raged at herself.

What a fool Jack must think her! Why couldn't she talk to him sensibly?

But then she remembered. Jack thought she was Kit – a boy, and just a stable lad at that, so it didn't matter what she said or didn't say. He was never going to pay her much heed.

But when Jack came into the ring with Opal, Kitty had to force herself not to stare. He was

23

such a brilliant horseman – he and Opal moved as one, in an effortless, flowing wave.

Kitty was on her last lap with Ginger when Sara Fanelli the tightrope walker appeared. On the ground and in her practice clothes, she looked less like a heavenly being, but she still moved with such grace that Kitty couldn't help gazing at her too.

As soon as Jack saw Sara by the tightrope kit, he made a beeline for her and jumped down from Opal to talk to her. Kitty was too far away to hear what he was saying, but she could tell from his face that it wasn't just a casual chat.

All the time Jack was talking, Sara kept her back turned to him and kept on checking her rope was in order. But then she swung round and said something that made Jack jump back onto Opal and ride off. From his grim face, Kitty could tell that he was angry.

She wondered what Sara had said to upset Jack so much. But she needed to focus on her stable tasks so Fred would give a good report of her to the guvnor, so she put Jack and Sara out of her mind.

Chapter 4
Jealous

It didn't take Kitty long to settle in and by the time they had packed up, moved on, unpacked and then packed again a time or two, she felt as if she'd been in the circus for ever. All the circus people were friendly, but she liked Fred and the guvnor's wife best. Ma Huxley, everyone called her, and she always had a kind word for Kitty.

The work was hard and tiring, but Kitty was only too happy to it. It was a joy to care for such splendid horses. The only thing that troubled her was that she still had no idea where Tom was. Fred asked around for her, but no one had heard of her brother.

If ever she had a spare moment during the day, Kitty sneaked into the big top to watch the performers practise or try out new routines. The person she most wanted to keep an eye on was Jack, but she liked watching Sara too, and it was easy to do both. Whenever Sara was in the ring, Jack was sure to be there, gazing up at her as she danced to and fro on her tightrope. He was in love with her – Kitty could tell from the wistful look on his face.

The thought made her heart twist.

But Kitty gave herself a good shake. It was no good getting silly about Jack. Compared to Sara, who was so beautiful, so poised, Kitty was nothing special. Even if Jack knew she was a girl he wouldn't give her a second look, and in any case that was never going to happen.

❧❧

But it turned out that Jack *had* been watching Kitty.

One day he caught her as she was leaving the ring. "Wait up, Kit," he said. "I want to ask you something. I've got an idea for a new act, but it means I'll have to train Opal to do some really difficult things. Will you help me?"

Kitty stared at him, astonished. "You want *me* to help?"

"Indeed I do." Jack grinned. "You have a way with horses. You understand them and they trust you."

Kitty blushed. "I'd love to," she said. "But I don't know if the guvnor –"

"I've already spoken to him," Jack said. "He says you can work with me for an hour or two every morning. What do you think?"

Kitty beamed at him. "When do we start?"

❦❦❦

Early the next morning Jack and Kitty met in the ring and Jack explained that he wanted to act out the story of Dick Turpin, the highwayman, and his loyal horse Black Bess.

"The crowd loves it," he said. "But in the story Black Bess dies of exhaustion after running for miles. That means we've got to teach Opal to lie down and stay still."

27

Kitty blew out her breath. "Tricky!"

"I know," Jack said. "But I reckon together we could do it."

To work with Jack every morning was like a dream come true and Kitty soon lost her shyness with him. But, as she discovered, he wasn't always the easiest person to be with.

One minute he would be as happy as a lark, and then he would sink into a pit of gloom in the blink of an eye. But Kitty forgave him his moods – she would have forgiven him anything. And he had good reason for his gloom because no matter what they tried, they couldn't get Opal to lie down.

One morning they were discussing what tactic to try next when a sneering voice broke in. "Still fooling about with that nag? You'll never get her to play dead, you know."

Kitty swung round. Oscar, the leader of the clowns, was standing there with a mocking smile plastered across his face.

Jack scowled. "I suppose you know all about horses," he snapped.

"Enough to know you're wasting your time." Oscar stalked off, still smirking.

"Don't take any notice of him, Kit," Jack said. "He's just jealous."

"Jealous?" Kitty said, surprised. "Why?"

"Oh, it doesn't matter," Jack said. He looked over to where Sara was practising somersaults on her rope. "Shall we stop now?"

Kitty was puzzled as she led Opal back to the stable tent. Jack had sounded so despondent. What did he mean about Oscar being jealous? And what did it have to do with Sara?

❦❦❦

After that, Kitty kept her eyes peeled for clues about Oscar and why he might be jealous.

She noticed that whenever Sara practised and Jack was in the ring, Oscar was there too. All the time he was working with the other clowns, he kept a close eye on the tightrope walker.

Was *he* in love with her too? It looked like it.

But Sara ignored everybody. If she was aware of Jack and Oscar, she gave no sign of it –

her focus was on her practice. Kitty suspected that Sara wasn't much older than her, but she seemed a lonely, rather sad creature, lost in a world of her own.

❧❧❧

One morning Jack passed Kitty a note and asked her to take it to Sara, who was practising on the other side of the ring.

Kitty stared at him. "You mean now?"

"Yes. Ask her to read it and bring me her answer."

Kitty was puzzled. Why didn't Jack speak to Sara himself? But then she remembered how Sara had acted that time he spoke to her. Perhaps he thought he'd have more success this way. Kitty walked over to the tightrope, aware of Oscar's eyes drilling into her back. "Hello?" she called up.

Sara stopped juggling and looked down at her. "Yes?" Her voice was cold.

"I have a note for you. From Jack."

"I don't want it."

30

"But you don't know what it says!" Kitty protested.

Sara made an impatient noise. "I can guess. Please tell your friend to stop bothering me." She tossed her hoops in the air and set off across the rope again.

Kitty stared after her. It was hopeless. She trailed back to Jack and shook her head.

Jack went quiet, but then he perked up. "Oh well. I'll try again when she's not practising. Come on, let's see if Opal will lie down today."

An hour later, Jack threw up his hands in despair. "This is hopeless, Kit. We'll have to give up on Dick Turpin."

Kitty was dismayed. Not work with Jack any more? Surely there must be something she could do.

"Why don't you let me have a go?" she asked. "Not here with all this going on. Some time when the ring's empty."

The next morning Kitty got up very early, took a bag of carrot chunks from the store and led Opal into the ring.

Every time Opal bowed her head, Kitty said, "Bow," and rewarded her with a chunk of carrot. Soon the bag of carrots was empty, and Opal had learned the command and lowered her head every time Kitty said it. Kitty knew she'd have to be patient, but now she knew Opal could learn. Every morning she got up before the other circus folk and, step by step, taught the horse to do what she wanted.

A month later, Kitty said to Jack, "How about you come and watch us tomorrow?"

"I'd rather stay in my bed," Jack grumbled. But he came, yawning and rubbing the sleep from his eyes. He watched as, at Kitty's signal, Opal lay down in the sawdust and stayed there, quite still.

"You've done it!" Jack clapped Kitty on the back. "We've got our Black Bess! Good work!"

Kitty blushed with pleasure. "Why don't you have a go?" she said.

She showed Jack the hand signal she'd used and, after a couple of tries, Opal lay down for him too.

Later on, when the ring was full, they tried again. The noise of the other performers distracted Opal and she refused to obey Jack's signal. Kitty tried standing where Opal could see her and, lo and behold, the mare lay down.

Jack punched the air. "We've done it! Dick Turpin will ride!"

Oscar was frowning over at them from across the ring. Jack gave him a gleeful wave.

Kitty couldn't stop smiling. If Tom were here he'd be so proud of her. But her smile faded fast as Jack pulled a note out of his pocket.

"Take this to Sara," he said. "Please? She'll be in her wagon after dinner."

Chapter 5
I cannot love him

That afternoon it rained. Kitty splashed to Sara's wagon through the wet and the mud, grumpy with Jack. This was sure to be a waste of time. Why didn't he just give up?

When Sara opened the door and saw Kitty dripping on the step, she frowned. "What do you want?"

"Can I come in?" Kitty said with a shiver. "Just for a moment."

Sara hesitated before stepping back and letting her visitor in. Kitty had been at the circus a while, but this was the first time she'd been in one of the wagons. She couldn't help staring round – it was all so neat and tidy.

"Well?" Sara's tone was chilly.

"I have a note for you. From Jack."

Sara flushed with anger. "I told you before. I don't want him bothering me."

Kitty just kept looking at Sara. In a low voice, she said, "I know you don't want anything to do with him. But you're making him very unhappy. Won't you at least read his note?"

Sara shook her head.

"He wants to meet you," Kitty said. "Why don't you do that? Then you can explain your feelings to him and perhaps he'll stop pestering you." She took the note out of her pocket and laid it on the table in front of them.

Sara stared back at her without speaking, but her expression had changed. It was softer now and she was looking at Kitty almost in wonder.

Kitty gave her a quick smile, then slipped away, closing the wagon door behind her.

Jack was waiting for her in the stable tent. "Well?"

"She's got the note," Kitty said. It was true, in a way.

"Excellent! Thank you!"

Kitty plucked up her courage. "You know, it might not turn out the way you want it to," she told him.

"It will," Jack said. "You've brought me luck, Kit. First Dick Turpin and now Sara."

Kitty bit her lip. She couldn't see Sara changing her mind, but Jack had no doubts – he'd bounced back into his cheery mood.

"Anyway, I have some more good news," he said. "I've spoken to the guvnor and told him Dick Turpin is ready. But I need you in the ring for the show and guess what? He said yes!"

"What?" Kitty said. "Why?"

"Without you, Opal won't lie down."

"But how can I be in the ring?"

"As a clown, of course." Jack sounded very pleased with himself.

"A clown! But how? I can't just stand there twiddling my thumbs."

"No, you'll have to learn a few tricks." Jack made it sound as if it was the easiest thing in the world.

Kitty was speechless. It was a ridiculous idea, and he hadn't even asked her first. But he was always like this, so caught up in what *he* wanted that he didn't think about anyone else. Then she had a horrible thought. "Oscar!" she said. "I won't have to work with *him*, will I?"

"Yes," Jack said, looking a bit sheepish. "Sorry. But –"

Kitty cut him off. "I won't do it, Jack. I can't."

"Please, Kit!" he begged. "I can't do Dick Turpin without you. And think of all the work we've done – it would be such a waste."

Kitty hesitated, but then she saw the pleading look in his brown eyes and she relented. "All right then, I'll try. But if I'm hopeless, that's it. I'm not going in the ring to make a fool of myself."

Jack beamed. "You won't be hopeless. Fred and I will help you and you'll be superb, I know you will."

Kitty didn't share his confidence, but deep down she knew that she'd do anything for Jack. She couldn't help herself.

❦❦❦

That night Kitty tossed and turned on her camp bed, long after the other stable lads had fallen asleep.

What had she been thinking? Why on earth had she agreed to Jack's idea?

She felt so restless that in the end she decided to go for a walk. She crept out of the tent and set off round the field. It was a beautiful night – the rain had passed over and thousands of stars glimmered in the inky sky. As she passed the animals' area, the bulk of the elephants loomed up in front of her, and she heard the rattle of their chains.

The next moment she jumped with fright as someone appeared from the stable tent. Then she saw that it was Jack, and she relaxed. She was about to speak to him, but as he came closer she saw the look of baffled fury on his face. She shrank back behind Nero's cage, grateful that the lion was asleep.

Jack stomped off into the darkness of the field, and then Kitty heard the sound of crying coming from inside the stable tent. She peeped in. Sara was sitting on a bale of straw with her head buried in her hands, and her back was shaking with sobs. Kitty crept over to join her on the bale and waited for the storm to pass.

After a while Sara blew her nose and wiped her face. She kept her head turned away, but she didn't get up and leave.

Kitty cleared her throat. "I'm sorry you're so unhappy," she said.

Sara looked at her then. "You are kind," she said. She sighed. "Jack is a nice boy, I can see that. He's handsome and talented and I think he means well, but –" She shrugged. "I took your advice. I told him that I don't love him, but he doesn't listen. How can I make him understand?"

"I don't know," said Kitty. "I could speak to him, if you like."

"You would do this for me?" Sara sounded surprised.

"Yes," Kitty said. "I'd like to help you."

Sara gave Kitty a long look then she lowered her eyes. "Jack is not the only reason I am sad," she said. She paused and then went on, "I had a brother, Carlo. We walked the tightrope together – a double act, you see."

Kitty nodded.

"But last year ... he fell." Sara bowed her head.

Kitty shivered. "He died?"

"Yes," Sara said simply.

There was a long silence. Kitty felt on the verge of tears herself. After a while she swallowed and said, "I'm so sorry, Sara." Then she said, "This is not the same – it is not a tragedy – but I think I understand a little of what you're feeling."

She sensed that Sara wanted her to go on.

"I have a brother. Tom," Kitty said. "Last year he ran away and we haven't heard from him since. I don't know whether I'll ever see him again." Her voice broke.

Sara took her hand and gave it a gentle squeeze. She didn't let go and the warm clasp was a comfort.

It was a relief to Kitty to share her grief about Tom, but she felt for Sara. At least Kitty still had hope – one day she might find Tom. But Sara really would never see her brother again.

"Why do you keep on with your act?" she asked Sara. "Aren't you afraid of falling too?"

Sara shrugged. "I don't know anything else. The tightrope is my life."

'And it could be your death,' Kitty thought with a shiver of fear. She hardly knew Sara, but she wouldn't want anything to happen to her.

Sara let go of Kitty's hand as she stood up. "It's late," she said. "We both need to sleep." She gave Kitty a shy look, not exactly a smile, but almost. "Thank you," she said.

Chapter 6
He's a very devil

The next day Jack started teaching Kitty how to be a clown. She hadn't forgotten her promise to Sara, but it didn't feel like the right time to speak to him about her.

Jack was a strict instructor. First he made her stretch and bend until her muscles hurt. "You're stiff because you've not done this before," he explained. "You need to be supple for tumbling."

"But I'm not going to be an acrobat!" Kitty protested.

"If you're a clown you'll be doing handsprings, flip-flaps, backflips, all of it ..." Jack laughed as Kitty's jaw dropped. "Also ... catch!" He tossed her an orange and then another and laughed again as Kitty fumbled and dropped them both. "And juggling, of course. Come on," he added in a kinder voice. "We'll start with cartwheels, they're not so tricky."

Kitty groaned. She'd had no idea what she was letting herself in for.

When Jack was busy, Fred took over. He didn't laugh at Kitty, but he was even more demanding.

Every night Kitty went to bed exhausted, but she couldn't get comfortable – whichever way she lay, her sore muscles complained. Often she felt she'd never get her body to do what she wanted it to, and she wept tears of frustration into her pillow. If she couldn't be in the ring as a clown, there'd be no Dick Turpin and Jack would be so disappointed in her.

"I'm never going to be able to do this," she wailed to Fred one morning as she collapsed out of another shaky handstand.

"You will," Fred said, and he offered his hand to help her up. "It just takes time."

Fred was right. After weeks of practice, Jack declared that Kitty was ready to work with Oscar. By now she could juggle up to five balls or hoops. She could manage backbends, cartwheels and handstands. She could even flip herself over, though she sometimes landed on her backside. But that didn't matter, Fred said. "It makes it funnier to watch," he told her.

Kitty didn't feel much like laughing herself – she was dreading working with Oscar. She'd watched him with the other clowns and he was just as much of a bully as she'd first thought. He could have helped Kitty while she was new to clowning, but instead he picked on her every chance he got.

Kitty was always on time, but Oscar would tap his big watch and snarl, "You're late." He made sure she was the butt of all the jokes – the one who was pushed over and had buckets of water chucked at her.

One morning, as Kitty stood there sore and soaking wet, he announced, "I have an idea for a new act. We fight with these swords." He passed Kitty a heavy wooden sword, with a cruel smile. "I will win, of course."

At that moment Sara came into the ring and passed Kitty on the way to her tightrope. "I've watched you," she said. "Every day you are a better clown. Stronger, more flexible – yes?" And she gave Kitty one of her rare, beautiful smiles.

It lit up her face like the sun coming out and Kitty's heart lifted. But the minute Sara walked off, Oscar raised his sword at Kitty and she shrank back.

"That's right," Oscar said. "Make it look as if you don't really want to fight."

That wasn't difficult. It was true!

And so Kitty darted about, trying to escape Oscar. She knew it must look funny because the other clowns were laughing, but her stomach was clenched with fear. Oscar was relentless, stabbing at her time and time again. Kitty swerved to avoid him and caught sight of Jack coming into the ring with Opal.

Smack! Something hit her hard on the side of the head and she found herself on the ground, stunned.

Oscar loomed over her. "Get up!" he barked.

"That's enough, Oscar," Jack said.

Oscar spun round to face Jack in a long moment of silence bristling with tension.

Then Sara was there, crouched beside Kitty. "Are you hurt?" she asked. "Can you stand?" She offered her hand and Kitty stood up.

She felt dizzy – her ear throbbed and her head felt as if a bomb had exploded inside it.

"Come," Sara said. "You can lie down in my wagon."

As they left the big top arm-in-arm, Kitty noticed Jack and Oscar scowling after them. She could understand Oscar's scowl, but why was Jack upset now?

❦❦❦

Sara made Kitty lie down on her bed and pulled up a stool next to her.

"Rest for a while," Sara said. "A blow to the head can be serious." She grimaced. "That Oscar – what a *mostro!*"

"I think it was an accident," Kitty said. "He's not that much of a monster ..."

Sara shook her head. "No. I was watching – he did it on purpose."

Kitty groaned. "Why does he hate me so much?"

"He hates everybody. Except himself." Sara patted Kitty's hand. "Perhaps he hates you because you are a friend of Jack."

"He doesn't like Jack?"

"Jack he hates most of all." Sara sighed. "Listen. I will tell you something but you must promise to tell no one."

"I promise," Kitty said.

"Oscar has a plan," Sara said. "He wants to leave Huxley's and start his own circus. He wants me to be in it. He thinks I will be a star." Her face twisted in disgust.

"You don't want to be star?"

"A star, yes, but not in any circus run by Oscar. The guvnor is a good man. Ma Huxley is very nice. This is a good place to be. But Oscar … No."

Kitty nodded. "But –" She frowned. "What has this to do with Jack?"

Sara snorted. "Oscar thinks I stay here because of Jack. Because I love him. Oscar is a fool. But enough of him." She waved her hand as if she wanted to brush away an annoying fly. "How do you feel now, Kit?"

"Better, thank you. My head still aches, but I'll survive."

"Good. Now you must go to the stable. No more clowning today."

Kitty took her advice. The last thing she wanted was to face Oscar again. But as she went down the steps of the wagon, Sara called after her. "Kit, be careful in the ring with Oscar. Perhaps he will try to hurt you again."

Chapter 7
Cruel

The next day Kitty's face was swollen, but Jack didn't even mention it. She was used to his ways by now, but still she felt hurt. When the Dick Turpin act went well, she expected him to be pleased, but he just said flatly, "That's it. When Oscar says you're ready, it goes in the show."

Kitty tried to find excuses for him. Perhaps he was upset about Sara.

Sara! Kitty remembered her promise to her new friend and felt guilty. Well, now was as good a time as any. Before she could change her mind, she said, "Jack, there's something I need to tell you ... about Sara."

Jack frowned.

Kitty rushed on. "I know how hard it must be, but you need to accept the truth. Sara doesn't love you. She'll never love you. Don't you think it would be better for you to forget her?"

"Better for *me*?" Jack spat the words out. "Are you sure you mean *me*?" And with that he spun on his heel and stalked off.

Stung, Kitty turned to Opal, who was waiting patiently by her side. "Oh, Opal," she whispered, "I was only trying to help."

The mare nuzzled her, pushing her beautiful face against Kitty's as if she understood.

❧❧❧

Jack's mood didn't pass. He was very cold towards Kitty, hardly saying a word to her as they practised together in the ring.

Fred noticed that Kitty was quieter than usual too. "Why the long face?" he asked one morning, as they were mucking out together. "What's wrong, Kit?"

Kitty wished she could tell him, but she couldn't. If she confided in Fred, he might see how much Jack meant to her.

"I'm worried about tonight," she said instead. That at least was true. The guvnor had been to watch her practise with the other clowns and he'd told Oscar that the act was ready. Tonight Kitty would take part in the show. The thought of it made her mouth go dry.

"I'm bound to make a fool of myself," she told Fred. "And everyone will be watching."

"You won't," Fred said. "And if you do, the crowd will think it's all part of the act."

※※※

In her baggy striped costume and with her face covered in white paint, Kitty waited with the other clowns by the entrance to the big top.

A cloud of butterflies was fluttering in her stomach, and as she heard the clowns' music start up, her heart missed a beat. But one of the other clowns cried, "Come on, Kit!" and grabbed her hand and the next moment she was out in the ring under the dazzling lights.

Kitty had no time to panic. The clowns launched into their act and she was swept along with them. She managed the juggling where, after she had shown her skill, she had to drop all five balls. She flew head over heels in a series of perfect cartwheels, and landed with her head in a bucket. Even the sword fight went well – she dodged Oscar so nimbly he never got near her.

All the time the crowd roared with laughter.

Kitty relaxed. They thought she was funny! It was going to be all right.

Then the guvnor's voice boomed out and Jack came bounding into the ring with Opal galloping beside him. Kitty's job was to hold the rope for Jack to jump over.

Kitty had seen him leap onto Opal's back dozens of times. But today, the moment he landed, the mare gave a scream of pain that made Kitty's blood run cold. Then Opal seemed to go mad. She bucked and tossed and jumped into the air. Jack hung on, but Opal reared up and flung him off.

Then she came crashing down on top of him.

Kitty forgot every rule of the circus she'd ever learned. She dropped the rope and dashed across the ring. Opal was back on her feet by now, trembling, but Jack lay still, his arm twisted at an angle that made Kitty's stomach turn.

Oscar was hissing something at Kitty, but she was frozen, staring in horror at Jack's white face.

"The horse!" Oscar snapped. "Take the horse!"

Kitty remembered with a jolt. If anything went wrong, she had to deal with the horses. Already the band was playing a jaunty tune and the other clowns were fooling about to distract the crowd.

As two ring hands carried Jack off on a stretcher, Kitty went to Opal and calmed her with soothing words until she could lead her out of the ring.

Fred was outside, his face nearly as white as Jack's. "I saw what happened," he said. "What scared Opal?"

Kitty was fighting to hold back tears. "Is Jack all right?"

"I don't know," Fred said, and Kitty saw that he was struggling not to cry too.

Together, they took Opal into her stall and Fred started to unbuckle the pad on her back. As he lifted it off, his face grew dark.

Under the pad, Opal's coat was matted with blood. A jagged splinter of broken glass stuck out of her back.

Kitty put her hand to her mouth. "No wonder she screamed and bucked like that. Poor Opal, she was in agony." She struggled to make sense of it. "I got her ready," she said at last. "That glass wasn't there then, I swear."

"Of course not," said Fred.

They stared at one another with shocked faces as the same thought struck them both.

Kitty felt sick. "Someone put it there on purpose," she said. "Someone wanted to hurt Opal ... and Jack too."

Chapter 8
Heart of flint

Kitty closed her eyes as Fred pulled the glass splinter out of Opal's back. He cleaned the cut with salt water and then offered the mare an apple. But Opal turned away from her treat.

"She'll be all right," Fred said, and he put the apple back in his pocket. "But no one can ride her for a while. Still –" His voice tailed away.

Kitty shivered. Was Fred thinking what she was? That Jack might not recover so well as the mare … She couldn't bear to think about it. With a heavy heart, she picked up the pad for Opal's back, but then turned as someone pushed through the canvas door. It was Jack!

He had his arm in a sling – but he was alive. Kitty felt shaky with relief.

Jack ignored her and went straight to Opal. "Is she all right?" he asked Fred.

"Yes," Fred said. "But look." He showed Jack the wound on Opal's back and the lethal splinter.

Jack's face was dark as a storm cloud as he rounded on Kitty. "You did this, didn't you!" he growled.

Kitty was struck dumb. Then his words sank in. "Me?" she cried. "No! Why would I do such a thing?"

"You know exactly why," Jack said. "You hate me because of Sara."

"What?"

"Admit it. You want to hurt me because you love her too."

"Jack, no! That's not true." Kitty's eyes filled with tears. How could she convince him? Apart from telling him the truth.

Jack's eyes glittered. "I don't want you near Opal again, do you understand? Fred, you'll see to that, won't you?"

After a quick, shocked glance at Kitty, Fred nodded.

Jack pushed past Kitty, but stopped at the door flap. "As for helping me with my act, Kit, forget it. I don't want you anywhere near me."

After he'd gone, there was a horrible silence. Fred shuffled his feet as if he didn't know what to say.

Kitty sank onto a bale of straw. She felt hollow and dazed. "Fred," she whispered. "It wasn't me."

Fred sat next to her and put his hand on her arm. "I know it wasn't."

Kitty stared at him. "You believe me?"

"Of course. I've seen how much Opal means to you. You'd never hurt her."

His trust made Kitty's eyes well up.

"But who would do such a cruel thing?" Fred said.

Kitty blinked back her tears. "It could have been Oscar."

"Oscar!" Fred's eyebrows shot up. "I know he's a bully. But hurt Opal? Why on earth would he do that?"

"I have an idea why," Kitty said. "But I can't tell you what it is. It's not my secret to share."

Fred's eyes met hers. "Is it to do with Sara?"

Kitty nodded.

"I thought so. You know," Fred said, "I left Opal near the entrance to the ring. Oscar could have slipped out and put the glass under the pad."

Kitty considered the idea. The more she thought about it, the more likely it seemed. She turned to Fred. "What if Oscar wants –" She swallowed. "What if Oscar wants to *kill* Jack? Suppose he tries again?"

Fred frowned. "We could keep watch on Jack," he said. "Make sure he's safe."

"That's a good idea. But, Fred …" Kitty's voice broke. "Jack doesn't want me anywhere near him."

"I'll do it," Fred said. "If I see anything, I'll tell you. And I'll tell Uncle Henry, too. Whoever it is, he'll sack them and then they won't be able to hurt Jack again."

"Your uncle might sack *me*," Kitty said. "When Jack tells him what he suspects."

"I don't think so," said Fred. "Uncle Henry likes you. And if I back you up, he'll believe me."

Kitty stayed sitting on the bale long after Fred had gone. A wave of homesickness came over her and caught her by surprise. She hadn't thought about Ma or Pa or Tom for ages. She didn't want to go home, but now she realised how much she missed them.

❧❦❦❧

Fred was right – the guvnor didn't sack Kitty. She was glad, but she missed Opal. And she missed Jack too – he wasn't speaking to her. If he came into the stable tent when she was there, he walked straight back out again.

Sara was offended on Kitty's behalf. "Jack is stupid," she said. "If he wasn't so wrapped up in himself, he would see that you would never hurt him or that lovely horse. But once he has an idea in his head ..." She sighed.

"I think he's blinded by his feelings for you," Kitty said. She couldn't work out why, but she still wanted to defend Jack.

"Pah!" Sara said. "These are not real feelings. He is, how do you say? Love-sick. No, I agree with the guvnor. I think the person who hurt Opal was one of those boys who creep into the big top without paying. They think life is a big joke."

Kitty wasn't convinced. She felt certain that someone in the circus was a threat to Jack.

❧❧❧

A few days later, Kitty was getting Ginger ready for the evening show when Fred came to find her.

"Come outside," he whispered.

Kitty followed him out of the tent. "What is it?"

Fred looked around to make sure they were alone. "I was chatting to Jack in his wagon this afternoon. While he was making us a cup of tea, I found this on the table under a newspaper. I'll slip it back when Jack's in the ring."

He handed Kitty a folded piece of paper. She opened it and read –

Dear Jack,

I have something important to tell you.

Meet me at the back of the stable tent at midnight tonight.

Sara

Kitty looked at Fred, her heart racing. "This isn't from Sara!" she said. "She wouldn't call Jack *dear*. And she wouldn't want to meet him. This is from someone else."

"The person who put the glass under Opal's pad?"

There was a moment's silence as they took this in. "Do you think we should be there?" Kitty said. "Just in case?" She tried to sound brave, but she could feel her legs shaking.

Fred nodded, and she saw the fear in his face too. "Tonight, then."

Chapter 9
Dead of night

Midnight. Kitty shivered as she and Fred kept watch, but not from cold.

They were hidden behind the bales of straw just inside the stable tent. The elephants were asleep, but Nero was pacing up and down his cage, growling and tossing his mane.

"Nero's restless tonight," Kitty whispered.

"I'd be restless if I was shut up in a cage all the time," Fred whispered back. "I think –" He held up his hand in warning.

Someone was coming.

It was Jack. In the moonlight, Kitty could see the eager look on his face. She groaned. He was expecting Sara – that was clear. But who would come instead? Her eyes never left the doorway. Fred was just as tense at her side.

A minute passed. Then another.

Jack had been pacing up and down, as restless as Nero, but now he stopped and looked across at the wagons, frowning. And then Kitty saw something happen behind Jack's back that made her heart leap into her throat.

The door of Nero's cage flew open.

For a second Nero crouched at the open door. Then, in a tawny blur, he sprang out of the cage and launched himself at Jack.

"Jack!" Kitty screamed. She leaped out of the tent and knocked Jack aside. At the same time she tried to twist herself out of Nero's way, but she had no chance – the lion turned on her and sank his vicious fangs into her leg.

Kitty heard Fred and Jack yell and curse as they grabbed pitchforks from the stable tent and prodded at Nero. At last the lion gave a great roar and let go, and Fred dragged Kitty away before he returned to help Jack drive Nero towards his cage.

Kitty lay on the ground unable to move. She was numb with shock and almost blacking out in pain. She heard Jack and Fred curse again and turned her head a tiny fraction to see Nero lope away towards the big top.

Then Fred was dashing out of the stable tent with a heavy brass bell, ringing it as hard as he could. Circus hands came running from every direction.

"Nero's out!" Fred cried as he pointed to the big top. "The lion's loose!"

One of the circus men snatched up a net from the stable tent and ran after the others.

Fred took off his shirt. "Here," he told Jack. "Use this to bind Kit's leg. I'll be back in a minute." He raced off.

With a grim face, Jack set to and bound the shirt round Kitty's leg. He wouldn't look at her and, when he'd finished, he walked off without a word.

Kitty's heart twisted. 'I've just saved his life,' she thought. 'Why is he being so cold?'

Next the guvnor arrived with a gaggle of circus folk and everyone gathered round Jack, all talking at once. Ma Huxley took one look at Kitty and rushed off. Sara sank down beside her and gave her a great hug.

"You are alive!" she cried. "Thank God!"

Kitty was grateful for Sara's kindness. She was still in shock and faint with pain, and Sara's warm arms were more comforting than any blanket.

Then Ma Huxley was back with her first aid bag. She shook her head over Kitty's leg before she began to clean it up.

Then the guvnor stepped forward. "Quiet, everyone!" he boomed. He nodded at his wife. "How's Kit?"

"Not so bad," Ma Huxley said. "He'll live. The wounds are deep, but the bleeding's stopped."

Just then the stable hands and Pablo the lion tamer came back with Nero in the net. He was snarling and trying to claw his way out, but they dragged him into his cage and Pablo locked the door. Then he turned to face everyone.

"Look!" He held up a length of rope. "This was no accident. Someone tied this to the door of Nero's cage and then unlocked it. Then they hid over by the store tent. When Jack came – one tug of the rope – and the lion was out!"

The crowd broke into uproar. The guvnor raised his hand for silence. "Who would do such a thing?" he demanded. "And how did they know you'd be here, Jack?"

Jack's face was dark as thunder as he stared at Kitty and Sara. "I was tricked," he said.

"Tricked? How?"

"Someone sent me a message to meet them here."

"Who?"

Jack pointed. "Kit!"

"No!" Kitty protested, her voice weak but steady. "It wasn't me." She had saved Jack's life and this was what he thought of her? After everything she'd done for him, all her loyalty and hard work, how could he possibly think she wanted to kill him?

She wanted to speak up for herself, but there was no fight left in her. To her annoyance, her eyes filled with tears. Sara had never left her side and now she squeezed Kitty's arm. Kitty gave her a wobbly smile of thanks.

"What makes you think Kit did this?" the guvnor asked Jack.

Jack hesitated. Then he said, "It's because of Sara."

"Me?" Sara cried, scrambling to her feet.

"Yes." Jack's face was flushed, but he went on. "Kit knows I love you. But he loves you too. So he wants me out of the way."

"No, Jack, you are wrong." Sara shook her head. "Kit is not like that. He has – how do you say it? – a noble soul."

Kitty blushed. A noble soul? How Tom would laugh if he heard that. She looked up and she saw Sara gazing down at her with a soft look in her eyes.

It hit Kitty like a bolt out of the blue. Had Sara fallen in love with *her*?

"Kit would never hurt you," she heard Sara declare to Jack. "Surely you can see that."

"Prove it then!" Jack challenged her.

Sara stared at Jack for a long moment, but then she turned away.

The next moment, Fred was pushing his way through the crowd. "I'll prove it!" he cried. "Kit would never hurt Jack ... Kit's a girl!"

A wild hubbub greeted this even more astonishing news.

Kitty shut her eyes. 'Oh, Fred,' she thought in dismay. 'What have you done?'

"I know who let Nero out," Fred shouted, and everyone fell silent once more. "And I suspect the same person put the glass under Opal's pad. It was Oscar!"

There was uproar.

"That's a very serious claim," the guvnor said to Fred when he'd managed to hush everyone again. "What proof do you have?"

"After Nero got out I spotted someone running away," Fred told his uncle. "I ran after them and I saw them hide in the fodder wagon. I locked the door. Then, on my way back, I found this by the store tent." He passed something to the guvnor that glinted in the moonlight.

As he examined it, the guvnor's face changed. "This is Oscar's watch," he announced in his booming ringmaster's voice. "And – look! – it's stopped at ten past twelve. That must be when he dropped it, running from Fred. That's all the proof I need."

He told two of the stable lads to check that it *was* Oscar in the fodder wagon. "If it is, keep him locked in there," he said. "He can stew till I'm ready for him."

Then the guvnor told them to get off back to their wagons. "Everything else can be sorted out in the morning," he said, wiping his forehead with a big hankie. "Off you go now. Bed!"

The circus people drifted off in groups, buzzing with gossip about the night's events. Jack kept looking back at Kitty as if he couldn't believe his eyes. As for Sara – she was still beside Kitty, gazing at her, open-mouthed.

In the end Ma Huxley managed to shoo her away and then she turned to Kitty.

"So –" she said. "What's your *real* name, my dear?"

"Kitty," Kitty said, shyly.

"Well, Kitty, I'm taking you to our wagon. You can stay with us while that leg heals. That'll be all right with you, Henry?"

"Whatever you say, my dear," the guvnor said.

Chapter 10
Spirit of love

Ma Huxley made Kitty stay in bed the next day, despite her protests.

"And no visitors," she added. "You've had more than enough excitement for now. You need to rest up, my dear!"

But when the guvnor had eaten his breakfast, he demanded to speak to Kitty. "No, Ma," he said when his wife protested. "The lass and me have some talking to do."

Kitty's stomach clenched with alarm. But then she saw the twinkle in his eye.

"You've been putting on a good show all this time," the guvnor said. "None of us suspected apart from Fred, and he's a canny lad. So what's it all about? Why were you pretending to be a lad?"

There was no point in keeping secrets any more, so Kitty took a deep breath and told the guvnor all about Tom and why she'd run away from home.

When she'd finished, he didn't say anything at first. Then he cleared his throat and Kitty crossed her fingers under Ma Huxley's patchwork bedcover.

"Well, Kit, I mean, Kitty," the guvnor said. "You're coming on nicely as a clown. And you're one of the best stable lads – or lasses – I've ever had. You've a remarkable understanding of those horses. So, if you want to stay and carry on as before, I'd be glad to have you."

Kitty could have kissed him. The guvnor didn't mind that she was a girl! She could stay with the circus and carry on doing what she loved.

"But what about Oscar?" she asked. "What's going to happen to him?"

"Don't worry about him," the guvnor said with a grimace. "I've already dealt with him."

And Kitty had to be content with that for now.

※※※

The next day Ma Huxley relented and let Fred come in to see Kitty. She was delighted – she'd already forgiven him for letting the cat out of the bag.

"Uncle Henry's sacked Oscar," he told her. "He's packed his bags and gone."

"Good riddance," Kitty said. "But what will happen to him?"

"Who cares?" Fred shrugged. "He isn't short of money. Perhaps he'll buy a ticket for a steam ship to America – there are lots of circuses there and they won't know he's not to be trusted."

"You know about Oscar's plan to start his own circus with Sara as its star?" Kitty said.

"Yes," Fred said. "Uncle Henry reckons that's why Oscar tried to kill Jack."

They were both quiet for a moment, thinking of what might have happened. Kitty brushed the thought aside and tapped Fred on the arm. "Why did you tell everyone I was a girl?" she asked.

"I thought it had gone on long enough," Fred said. "And it was the only way to get it into Jack's fat head that you weren't trying to kill him."

"But how did you know?" Kitty asked.

"I guessed when your pa came looking for you."

"As long ago as that! You never said anything."

"It's none of my business, is it?" Fred said with a shrug. "You've fitted in all right and you're a genius with the horses – and that's what counts."

Before Kitty could say anything, Ma Huxley bustled in. "That's enough for today, young man," she said and shooed Fred out.

Kitty didn't object – she was ready for a rest. As Ma Huxley fussed around her, she was happy to lie back and think what a true friend Fred was.

He'd talked to her in just the same way as usual. At least with him, nothing had changed.

Kitty was less sure how things would be with Jack and Sara. How would they feel about her hoodwinking them? And how did she feel about them now? She really wasn't sure at all.

❧❧❧❧

When Sara arrived with a bunch of purple violets, Kitty's heart leaped.

But Sara wasn't smiling. "These are for you," she said in her old, crisp way and she thrust the posy into Kitty's hand.

Kitty winced. Had Sara not forgiven her? To hide her confusion, she buried her nose in the violets and breathed in their sweet scent. A haunting tune drifted over from the big top and seemed to echo what Kitty was feeling – a painful longing she couldn't explain.

The next moment Sara threw her arms around her in a warm hug.

Kitty's eyes filled with tears of relief. "You're not cross?" she said. "That I let you think I was a boy?"

Sara gave her a funny little smile. "I am a little disappointed, I have to say. You make … how shall I put it? … a *bellissimo* boy. But also, a very nice girl." She gazed at Kitty for a long moment.

Kitty couldn't look away and something passed between them like an electric spark that made Kitty catch her breath. She couldn't tell whether it was excitement she was feeling or fear. Whatever was wrong with her?

But then Sara laughed and broke the spell. "I tease you, Kitty. The important thing is – we are still friends, yes?"

Kitty nodded and did her best to smile back. "Of course."

"Good. Friends, they are for always. Now," Sara said, brisk again. "My tightrope calls me. I must go and practise. But I will come again, very soon." She gave Kitty a funny half-salute and was gone.

Kitty lay in her bed, stunned. Had that really happened or had she imagined it? If it was a dream, it would be lovely to sleep and dream some more.

The next day after dinner, Ma Huxley said, "It's time you were out and about, Miss Kitty. The sun's shining and you need to exercise that leg of yours. But don't overdo it, mind."

Kitty did as she was told and limped her way down the wagon steps. Then she half hobbled, half ran to the stable tent and Opal.

"Oh, Opal," Kitty said, patting the mare. "Hello ... hello again." Opal nickered softly in greeting and nuzzled Kitty. But then she lifted her head and they both turned to find Jack standing there, looking rattled.

And in that moment Kitty knew how she felt about him. Only a few days ago, her heart would have raced at the sight of him. But now she realised that those old feelings had died. Jack had killed them – he'd failed to see how much she cared for him, he'd even believed that she wanted to kill him.

And she saw too that those feelings were like glistening cobwebs spun from his charm and the magic of his horsemanship and his dark good looks that reminded her of Tom. Her feelings for him had been nothing but love-sickness, just as he had been love-sick with longing for Sara. None of it was real.

She waited to see what he had to say.

Jack shuffled his feet. Then he blurted out, "I've been so horrible to you, Kit, er, Kitty. And I just wanted to say ... well ... I'm sorry."

Kitty nodded. "It was my fault too," she said. "You know, pretending to be a boy."

He waved his arm as if to brush that aside. "No, the thing is – I should have trusted you. I can see now what a good friend you've been to me – all that work you put into Dick Turpin and then the business with Sara –"

He broke off and shook his head.

"You were right," he went on. "I can see that now. I was a fool to think I could make her love me, when she clearly doesn't. So –" He shrugged and gave one of his charming smiles. "I'm doing my best to forget her."

Kitty felt oddly relieved. But was that for his sake or her own?

"Kitty …" Jack looked at her with another dazzling smile. "I don't suppose you'd be interested in … um … taking a walk with me?"

Kitty gave a snort of laughter which she tried to turn into a cough. He was so *fickle*. No sooner had he given up on Sara than he had his eye on her! His cheek was astonishing but she couldn't help being fond of him and she didn't want to be mean. "That's kind of you, Jack," she said, "but no, thank you."

His face fell, but only for a moment. "Oh, well – no walks," he said. "But apart from everything else, you saved my life! Is there *anything* I can do to thank you?"

Kitty knew her answer in an instant. "Yes. I want us to do the Dick Turpin act together."

Jack's face broke into a grin. "You do? After everything that's happened?"

Kitty nodded.

"Of course we'll do it, then."

"And I'd like to go back to caring for Opal."

"Are you still going to work here in the stables?" he asked, surprised. "I mean, it's not what most girls would do."

"I'm not *most girls*," Kitty said.

"You're certainly not." Jack laughed. "And I'd be delighted if you'd look after Opal. I think she's missed you."

Kitty wanted to jump for joy. But instead she said, "Good, that's settled then."

Chapter 11
Surprise

By the end of the month, Kitty's leg had healed enough for her to take up her tasks in the stable tent and, a few weeks after that, she was ready to try her ring acts again.

Now he'd got over his two disappointments in love, Jack seemed more relaxed, and his moodiness and bad temper were quite gone. He and Kitty made a good team and they soon felt ready for the Dick Turpin act.

The clown act was another matter. It was like starting all over again. Kitty's body had stiffened up and even simple bends and stretches were an effort. She was groaning with pain and tiredness, ready to give up, when Sara appeared.

"We do it together," Sara announced. "It goes better so."

And she was right. With Sara at her side, Kitty worked hard and her confidence grew. It wasn't long before she was tumbling and juggling with an ease she'd never had before.

"Do you know," she said to Sara one morning, "I never thought I'd say it, but I'm actually enjoying all this now!"

Sara smiled. "Good." She put her head on one side. "You are ready now, I think, to join the other clowns. But have you ever thought of the tightrope, Kitty?"

Kitty gaped at her. "Me?"

"Why not?" said Sara. "If you can do it on the ground, it's not so difficult in the air. You should try. I'll help you."

It had never crossed her mind, but now Kitty thought about it, performing on the tightrope was a thrilling idea. Scary, with its risk of falling, but how wonderful to share it with Sara.

"If it goes well," Sara went on, "who knows? Perhaps one day we could be a double act."

Kitty thought her heart was going to burst with joy. All she could do was grin like a fool.

Sara laughed at her. "Now, back to work," she said, pretending to be stern, "or this dream of ours will never happen."

❧❧

When at last the circus made its way round to Kitty's home town, she could hardly believe a year had passed. But as they travelled along the streets she knew so well, Kitty began to feel homesick. She was due to perform in the ring for the first time since her injury and she was fretting in case someone in the audience spotted her.

When she told Fred this, he laughed. "No one will know you, silly! Not in your clown costume."

At show time, Kitty waited outside the entrance to the big top, as sick with nerves as she'd been the first time. But then Sara appeared at her side. She squeezed Kitty's hand and whispered, "You can do it! You're a star!"

Sara's words made all the difference. Kitty sailed through her performance and at the end she basked in the cheers of the crowd, enormously thrilled and relieved.

After the show, Kitty ran back into the ring to help the others tidy up. Sara dashed over and gave her a big hug. "See?" she said. "I was right!"

Kitty clung to Sara, her heart full. "I couldn't have done it without you."

"Nonsense," Sara said, holding her close. "You just need to believe in yourself – and your talents – more." She gazed into Kitty's eyes and Kitty's heart hammered like a steam engine.

Someone coughed.

She looked round to see the guvnor standing close by. "When you've finished, Kitty, I'd like a word with you."

Kitty felt herself blush scarlet and she let go of Sara at once. But the guvnor didn't seem to notice that she was flustered. He grasped her hand.

"Well done, lass," he said. "That was a stunning performance." He beamed at her. "Now, I've a surprise for you. Come with me."

Kitty followed the guvnor. A surprise? What could it be? And then she stopped dead.

Ma and Pa.

She looked again and her heart skipped a beat.

"Tom!" she cried.

She raced over to her family. She hugged Tom, Ma hugged her, Kitty laughed and cried at the same time, and they all tried to talk at once.

When Kitty broke free at last, she saw Pa standing off to one side. She hesitated, but then she saw the tears in his eyes. Without a word, he held out his arms. She ran to him and buried her face in his chest. He stroked her short hair and murmured, "Kitty, oh my Kitty."

And she realised that she'd got it all wrong. Pa had lashed out at her because he was so upset about Tom. He didn't hate her at all.

She felt as if a great weight had been lifted off her.

All the while, the guvnor had been standing by. Kitty turned to him with tears in her eyes. "You're a magician. How did you get them here?"

"Well, lass, there's no magic involved," the guvnor said. "I tracked down your parents and invited them. I told them you'd be in the show, and they couldn't resist. Now then," he went on. "Ma Huxley has laid on a bite of supper in our wagon and you're all welcome. It seems to me you've a deal of catching up to do."

Chapter 12
What's to come

It was a tight fit inside the Huxleys' wagon. Ma Huxley had invited Jack, Fred and Sara to supper as well. Kitty sat in a daze, squashed between Fred and Tom. Her head was buzzing with questions.

As they ate and talked, the answers came.

A few months ago Tom had written to Ma and Pa. "I've been in a circus too," he told Kitty. "Beal's, it's called."

"I guessed as much!" Kitty cried. "Are you a trick rider? Like Jack?"

"I'm not as good as Jack yet." Tom laughed. "But I'm getting there."

Tom and Jack smiled at one another and Kitty could see that they would get on well. "But why didn't you write sooner?" she asked. "We were all so worried."

Tom's smile faded and he looked ashamed. "I know, I'm sorry. But I wanted to wait to see whether I'd be a success. As a circus rider, I mean." He looked at Pa.

"And are you?" Kitty asked. "Will you stay in the circus?"

Tom nodded. He grinned, but Kitty didn't know why. "What about the stables, Pa?" she asked. "How will you manage without Tom?"

Pa looked embarrassed. "As soon as Tom wrote to us, I realised I was being daft – I didn't have to do it all myself. I've got two new lads working with me now."

Kitty was glad. But then a horrid thought struck her. Now that they'd found her, would Ma and Pa insist that *she* went back home with them?

The guvnor noticed that she'd gone quiet. "What's the matter, lass?"

Kitty hesitated. She felt shy about saying it in front of everyone, but she had to know. "What's going to happen to me, now?" she asked.

"I think your pa has something to say about that."

Kitty fixed her eyes on Pa and he smiled at her. "Well, Kitty," he said, "your ma and I had a chat with Mr Huxley this afternoon. He said perhaps we should watch the show before we made up our minds. You did well, lass. In fact, you were wonderful."

"You were, my love," Ma put in, beaming at her.

Kitty's heart swelled. Ma and Pa wouldn't say that unless they meant it.

"So your ma and me have decided," Pa said. "It's up to you, lass. That's what we've said to Tom, too. It's only fair. If you want to come home, well ... you know how happy we'd be. But we can see you've made some good friends here. And, like Tom, you've found a life that makes you happy. So, if you want to stay, we'd understand."

There was a silence. Everyone's eyes were fixed on Kitty, waiting for her to decide.

She looked from Ma to Pa. She loved them so much and now that Pa was happy again, it would be lovely to be at home with them.

Then she looked at the Huxleys, at Jack and Fred, all smiling at her too. They were like a second family to her.

Last she looked at Sara, gazing at her across the table.

Kitty swallowed. She felt torn, but in her heart she knew what she wanted to do.

"I'd like to stay here with Huxley's Circus." She smiled. "After all, it is the greatest show of all …"

"Hoorah!" cried Fred. "Bravo!" And he raised his cup in a toast.

Jack beamed and, from across the table, Sara gave her one of her wonderful smiles.

"I'll come and see you as often as I can," Kitty told her parents. "And I'll come home for the winter break, if that's all right."

"Of course it is, my love," said Ma. "Come whenever you like – you'll always be welcome."

"Good, that's decided then," the guvnor said. "Now, I had a chat with young Tom here this afternoon as well. It seems he's not altogether happy at Beal's. I'm not surprised. It's a feeble sort of outfit –"

"Henry!" Ma Huxley broke in. "Get to the point."

"Yes, dear," the guvnor said. "Well, Tom's shown me what he can do and I've offered him a job with us. Of course he accepted. I mean, who'd say no to Huxley's instead of Beal's with their –"

Ma Huxley gave him another look, and he went on. "Well, yes. I reckon Tom and Jack will make a fine double act and Jack agrees."

Kitty threw her arms round her brother. "Oh Tom, that's splendid. We can work with the horses together."

Tom laughed and ruffled her hair. "Yes. It'll be just like the old days. Only you seem to wear trousers now. In fact, aren't they *my* old trousers you've got on?"

"So, now that's all settled," said Ma Huxley, "who wants a slice of my apple pie?"

Everyone set to and a buzz of chatter broke out.

Kitty didn't join in.

She sat in a daze of joy, seeing her future stretch in front of her like a golden path – full of hope and possibility.

Her eyes met Sara's across the table and they smiled at one another.

About *The Greatest Show of All*

My story is inspired by *Twelfth Night* by William Shakespeare.

I decided to set it in a circus in the past because a circus is an enclosed world, like the world where *Twelfth Night* takes place. It's a magical place, where people dress up and perform. It's also a place where you feel anything can happen, a place of excitement, tension and laughter.

In *Twelfth Night*, a girl called Viola decides to dress as a boy and this creates comical confusion. When a Duke called Orsino sends Viola to woo Olivia with his love messages, Olivia falls in love with Viola, which is not at all what Orsino intends. And Viola falls in love with Orsino, but of course she has to keep this to herself.

This idea of a love triangle – with a girl dressed as a boy – lies at the heart of my story, too.

When Kitty runs off to join Huxley's circus – 'the greatest show on earth' – she turns herself into Kit and this disguise leads to a tangle of feelings involving Jack and Sara. Kitty has to put on a show, not just as a circus clown, but also by acting the part of a boy. And she is putting on a show in her dealings with others, because she has to learn to hide the true feelings of her heart.

The part of the story that features Oscar is my own invention. He is closest to a character called Malvolio in *Twelfth Night*. Both Malvolio and Oscar think highly of themselves, cast a shadow over the romance and add to the confusion.

Kitty sets off on her adventure, hoping to find her brother Tom and to follow her own dreams. Along the way, she makes unexpected discoveries about herself and others. Like the characters in *Twelfth Night* she also has to answer the all-important question, "Where does my heart truly lie?"

Our books are tested
for children and young people by
children and young people.

Thanks to everyone who consulted on
a manuscript for their time and effort in
helping us to make our books better
for our readers.

PERFECT CAKES
EVERY TIME

PERFECT
CAKES
EVERY TIME

Victoria Combe

RIGHT WAY

Constable and Robinson Ltd
3 The Lanchesters
162 Fulham Palace Road
London W6 9ER
www.constablerobinson.com

Originally published as *Foolproof Cake Recipes* by Robinson Publishing 1998.
Selection and editorial material © *The Daily Telegraph* 1998.
Textual copyright © Various. Illustrations © Slatter-Anderson.
This edition published by Right Way,
an imprint of Constable & Robinson, 2009.

Every effort has been made by the Publishers and *The Daily Telegraph*
to contact each individual contributor. If any recipe has appeared
without proper acknowledgement, the Publishers and *The Daily Telegraph*
apologise unreservedly.

A copy of the British Library Cataloguing in Publication Data
is available from the British Library

ISBN: 978-0-7160-2215-2

CONTENTS

INTRODUCTION

Fresh back from honeymoon – with sand still in my shoes – my husband John announced that his parents were coming for afternoon tea. I blanched. Tea meant baking cakes – a foreign and mysterious process that I had never dared attempt.

Quivering over my shiny new kitchen scales, I set about making ginger nuts because the recipe claimed they could not fail. But they could – and they did. I had to hide the humiliating brown splodges glued to the baking tray and resort to a box of Mr Kipling.

Knowing that this must not happen again, I appealed for help in a column to readers of *The Daily Telegraph*. Their response was wonderful. I received tried and tested recipes which had been family treasures through the generations, and through both world wars. Given such encouragement, I set about learning how to bake cakes and I am still doing so.

But this book is not about my own misadventures with baking tins. It is founded on the wisdom of readers who were generous enough to impart their own recipes for easy-to-make delicious cakes which have wooed in-laws, difficult children and even members of the W.I. Inspired by such riches, I felt moved to go back to the mixing bowl.

I began with a Moist Lemon Cake (page 140) from Pam Daniels, of Norwich, which she claimed 'went down a bomb' with the W.I. and had been a favourite of her late husband, who died just before their Golden Wedding Anniversary. Mrs Daniels insisted on free-range eggs. Admittedly, I was a bit cack-handed at grating the lemon, but coped well with measuring and wielding the food processor. I had to wait 40 minutes for the outcome, but it was worth it. I opened the oven door to see a risen, golden cake. My spirits soared.

I marvelled at the number of women who are so proficient in the art of cake-making. In this age of women's emancipation, we are expected to be coy about homely skills. The very idea of a woman in her pinny turning out a perfect cherry cake amounts to incorrect thinking. Nonetheless, when my cry for help went out, readers rallied with enthusiasm. They seemed to rejoice at the thought that a newly-married woman might worry about the contents of a cake stand before offering tea to her mother-in-law.

I held a mini-contest on readers' recipes in our Wiltshire kitchen with two little boys who live nearby acting as judges. I made six cakes, all of which claimed to be idiot-proof. They all came off, but Mrs Daniels' Moist Lemon Cake was voted a clear winner by Harry, six, and his three-year-old brother Marcus.

The runners-up also appear in this book. There is a splendid Chocolate Truffle Cake (page 110) from Ann Meddings, of Kingston in Surrey, which works well as a pudding served with crème fraîche and a few summer berries on the side, and a Sticky Ginger Cake (page 20) from Barbara Jackson, of Penicuik in Midlothian.

It was Mrs. Jackson, generously imparting her mother's secret cake recipe, who warned me that home-bakers were a 'very evangelising species'. One mouthful of her Sticky Ginger Cake and my face shone with the look of a new convert.

I have learned, to my astonishment, that I find sweet pleasure from seeing a freshly-baked cake standing proud on a baking tray. I know it is not what is expected of a young woman on a Sunday afternoon, when there is paragliding and deep-sea diving on offer. Yet in a funny sort of way it is exciting and there is plenty of risk. As Adam Lindsay Gordon had it:

'There is no game that is worth a rap
For a rational man to play
Into which no accident, no mishap
Can possibly find its way.'

So here I am, the new evangelist. I cannot yet pretend to know all about baking, and I learn more with every cake. But what the authors of these recipes offer is a wealth of knowledge which I hope may inspire other novices like me to dabble in the mixing bowl.

A warning note: there is a lot of kit involved. There seems no limit to the choice of baking tins. And when it comes to the ingredients, I quake at the variety of flours and sugars on offer. My humble advice is to keep your eye on the kitchen scales. My sister Rachel, who helped to build my confidence in early baking days, advised me that baking was essentially a science. If the chemistry was to work, she said, I needed to be precise in my measurements. Experienced cooks may use a pinch of this and a handful of that. Novices cannot.

Rachel gave me an American Pound Cake recipe (page 45) which she inherited from her great grandmother-in-law from Louisiana. Rachel made this rich, buttery cake for us at home and it was devoured by our three brothers before it had time to cool in the tin. It is a big, hearty cake for hungry chaps.

My mother-in-law, Pam Whitwam, who involuntarily started the whole thing rolling, has considerately passed on her brilliant Chocolate Cake recipe (page 115) which kept her two sons very happy and which husband John chose for his birthday cake when a child. My first attempt won modified praise. Not quite as good as Mum made.

Never mind. Novices have to start somewhere. This is meant to be a vote of thanks to so many correspondents who encouraged me to travel down the wiggly road towards perfect cake making.

Thank you.

Victoria Combe

1
CAKE KNOW-HOW

Do not be put off by the formidable baking sections in supermarkets, which are always surrounded by brisk, efficient shoppers whom you would never dare ask for advice. Here is a crash course in ingredients which will help you bluff your way to the checkout, unscathed.

Flour
Some people rely on self-raising for every cake, others are fussier about the flours they use.

There are two types: high-gluten (strong) and low-gluten (weak). A strong flour, which is used in bread making, has a gluten content of 10–15 per cent, which gives it good raising power and a light, open texture. A soft flour, with a low gluten content of 7–10 per cent, absorbs fat well, gives a smaller rise and a finer texture, and is best for most cakes and biscuits.

Choosing between plain and self-raising is like choosing between an automatic and a geared car. The 'automatic' flour gives you a good balance of raising agents, but with plain flour you can control what you add. The general advice is $2^1/_2$ teaspoons of baking powder to every 250 g/8 oz plain flour.

Sifting flour makes it easier to mix. Some stalwart bakers swear that sifting flour leads to a lighter cake.

Sugar
Go for caster sugar for sponge cakes, and if you have run out and are desperate, you can always whizz some granulated in a liquidiser/food processor for a similar effect.

Soft brown sugar, dark or light, gives a caramel flavour and is best in ginger cakes and fruit cakes.

Demerara sugar is coarser than granulated and is suitable in cakes where the ingredients are heated before baking so that the sugar dissolves.

Other sweeteners

Treacle gives a lovely dark colour to chocolate, ginger and fruit cakes. It is not as sweet as its blonde sister, golden syrup, which goes well in cakes with spices, such as cinnamon, allspice and nutmeg. Both give a good sticky texture.

Honey is an excellent sweetener, but keep in mind that it is sweeter than sugar. It has a distinctive flavour and also has the great advantage of keeping cakes fresher for longer.

Fat

Most cakes are made with butter or margarine, though some use oil, which is easy to mix but has a rather flat taste. Some people insist that butter tastes better and is worth the extra expense. Do not use butter or margarine straight from the fridge.

Fruit

Dried fruit should be plump and soft. If it has gone horrible and hard, soak it in hot water for a few minutes and drain on kitchen paper.

Eggs

The debate over whether to use free-range eggs or ordinary eggs is complicated and I will not attempt to enter into the right/wrong row over how the chickens are kept. I do know that free-range eggs taste better and have a richer colour, but they cost more.

Be careful when using recipes with raw eggs. The risk of salmonella means that they should not be given to pregnant and nursing mothers, small children or the elderly.

Nuts

Everyone knows the risks of nut allergies and the need to tell people if a cake has any trace of nuts in its ingredients. For some people with an allergy, even touching a walnut on top of a cake could cause a life-threatening reaction. In the light of this, it is advisable not to give cakes containing nuts to very small children without consulting their parents beforehand.

Measurements
Both metric and imperial measurements are given in the recipes. Either is fine, but do not mix the two, as they do vary very slightly.

Standard level spoon measurements are used throughout.
1 tablespoon = 15 ml
1 teaspoon = 5 ml

Preparing the cake tins
First of all, invest in a good variety of tins: two sandwich, one deep tin with a loose bottom, a bun tray, a muffin tray, loaf tins both big and small and a ring tin for special celebration cakes.

Grease the cake tins lightly with softened butter or margarine – preferably unsalted – or you can use oil. Then line the tin with greaseproof paper, which also needs to be thoroughly greased.

For fruit cakes, you need to line the whole tin. You could make the liners yourself if you are a sucker for punishment, or you can buy them in bulk. I use Lakeland, which have an efficient mail order service (www.lakeland.co.uk).

Sponge cakes need only be lined on the bottom of the tin – ready-cut discs of paper can be bought, or made at home. You will be able to use that school compass again.

With a very rich fruit mixture, which needs a long cooking time, it is a good idea to put a double strip of thick brown paper around the outside of the tin. This helps prevent the outside of the cake overcooking.

Baking cakes
Ovens should always be preheated to the temperature stated in the recipe. If you have a fan-assisted oven, follow the manufactur-

er's instructions for adjusting times and temperatures. It is usually advisable to shave off five to seven minutes from the time, but no two cookers are exactly the same.

When a cake is cooked, it should be well risen, golden brown, and starting to shrink away from the sides. You can pierce the cake with a skewer and if it comes out clean, with no traces of mixture, the cake is ready.

It can be difficult to tell when a cake is cooked. Another way to do this is to press the centre of the top of the cake lightly with a finger. It should feel spongy, give slight resistance to the pressure, and bounce back quickly, leaving no fingermark.

2
SPONGE CAKES

CARROT CAKE

250 g/8 oz butter
375 g/12 oz demerara sugar
finely grated rind of 1
  orange
4 eggs
300 g/10 oz plain flour
$^1/_2$ teaspoon nutmeg
1 teaspoon cinnamon
1 teaspoon bicarbonate of
  soda

5–6 medium carrots, grated
175 g/6 oz walnuts, chopped
75 ml/3 fl oz warm water
3 teaspoons baking powder
$^1/_2$ teaspoon salt

❶ Grease and line the base of a 23 cm/9 inch round, high-sided cake tin. Preheat the oven to 180°C/350°F/Gas Mark 4.

❷ Cream together the butter, sugar and orange rind. Add the eggs and sift in the flour.

❸ Then add the nutmeg, cinnamon, bicarbonate of soda, grated carrots, chopped walnuts, warm water, baking powder and salt. Now give the mixture a really good stir.

❹ Put the cake mixture into the prepared cake tin and bake in the preheated oven for 1 hour 10 minutes, or until the top springs back when pressed lightly.

❺ Allow the cake to cool in the tin for 5 minutes, then turn out on a cake rack and allow to cool completely.

Tony Hogger
Blackshots, Grays

'Carrot cake's a wonderful thing. You can kid yourself that it's healthier than other cakes and eat several slices without feeling in the least bit guilty.'

Preparation Time: 40 minutes
Cooking Time: 1 hour 10 minutes
Oven Temperature: 180°C/350°F/Gas Mark 4

Reader's Tip: A delicious topping for carrot cake is to mix cream cheese with lemon juice and cover the cake with this.

GRANNY'S NO-FAIL SPONGE

3 eggs, separated
75 g/3 oz caster sugar
75 g/3 oz self-raising flour,
  sifted with $1/2$ teaspoon
  baking powder
raspberry jam
double cream, whipped with
  a little caster sugar

❶ Grease and flour two 18 cm/7 inch cake tins and pre-heat the oven to 200°C/400°F/Gas Mark 6.

❷ Whisk the egg whites until stiff but not dry. Now add the caster sugar and whisk again to get a glossy finish.

❸ Drop in the egg yolks in three different places and whisk for 1 minute.

❹ Fold in the sifted flour and baking powder, using a metal spoon.

❺ Turn the mixture into the prepared cake tins and bake in the preheated oven for 15 minutes, or until the edges begin to shrink away from the sides. Allow to cool on a cooling rack. Sandwich the two cakes together with raspberry jam and whipped cream.

Emma Gardner
Newtonabbey, Northern Ireland

Preparation Time: 15 minutes
Cooking Time: 15 minutes
Oven Temperature: 200°C/400°F/Gas Mark 6

Reader's Tip: This is a fat-free sponge, which is easier on the tummy – if you don't load on the double cream. When you separate the eggs, try to keep the yolks whole so as to stop any yolk getting into the white.

STICKY GINGER CAKE

300 g/10oz self-raising flour
200 g/7 oz soft light brown
  sugar
125 g/4 oz butter or
  margarine
$^3/_4$ teaspoon bicarbonate of
  soda
2 teaspoons ginger powder
2 tablespoons golden syrup
1 egg
250 ml/8 fl oz milk

❶ Grease and line a 14 x 24 cm/6 x 9$^1/_2$ inch rectangular baking tray, or a 20 cm/8 inch square baking tray. Preheat the oven to 180°C/350°F/Gas Mark 4.

❷ Put all the ingredients except the milk into a mixing bowl.

❸ Heat the milk to boiling point. Pour the hot milk into the bowl, and mix well until really smooth.

❹ Pour into the prepared tin and bake in the preheated oven for 30 minutes or until the top springs back when pressed.

5 Leave to cool for 10 minutes before turning out on to a cooling rack.

Barbara Jackson
Penicuik, Midlothian

Preparation Time:	10 minutes
Cooking Time:	30 minutess
Oven Temperature:	180°C/350°F/Gas Mark 4
Reader's Tip:	All the ingredients should be at room temperature before use. Do not try to use margarine or butter straight from the fridge.

CHERRY LAYER CAKE

150 g/5 oz self-raising flour
125 g/4 oz caster sugar
1 teaspoon baking powder
2 large eggs
7 tablespoons cooking oil
2 tablespoons milk
1 teaspoon vanilla essence
125 g/4 oz glacé cherries,
quartered

❶ Grease and line two 18 cm/7 inch cake tins or, if you prefer, use 20 little cake cases. Preheat the oven to 200°C/400°F/Gas Mark 6.

❷ Sift together the flour, sugar and baking powder.

❸ Add the eggs, oil, milk, vanilla essence and glacé cherries. Beat well, using a wooden spoon, or a hand or electric mixer, until all the ingredients are well blended and the mixture is smooth.

❹ Divide the mixture between the two prepared cake tins, or the 20 little cake cases. Bake the large cakes for 20 minutes, or the small ones for 10–15 minutes, until the cakes are well risen and springy to the touch.

5 Fill and ice the cakes as you wish.

Gillian and Yvonne
Darlington, County Durham

'This is my mainstay for speed
and variety, as the flavourings you
use can be varied according to taste.
It's honestly impossible to spoil:
idiot-proof, and husband-, student
daughter- and bachelor
brother-proof too.'

Preparation Time:	15 minutes
Cooking Time:	10–20 minutes
Oven Temperature:	200°C/400°F/Gas Mark 6
Reader's Tip:	This mixture is much more liquid than the creamed mixture you need for a Victoria sponge – more like a thick batter. If you use individual cake cases, it's a good idea to place these in deep bun tins to help them keep their shape.

ORANGE SNOW CAKE

150 g/5 oz margarine
75 g/3 oz caster sugar
2 eggs, separated
250 g/8 oz self-raising flour
2 tablespoons marmalade
rind and juice of 1 orange
icing sugar, for dusting

❶ Grease and line the base of an 18 cm/7 inch round, deep-sided cake tin with greaseproof paper. Preheat the oven to 190°C/375°F/Gas Mark 5.

❷ Cream together the margarine and sugar, then add the egg yolks. Sift in the flour, and stir in the marmalade, the orange rind and 4 tablespoons of the juice.

❸ Whisk the egg whites until stiff. Fold in a couple of tablespoons of egg white, then fold in the rest.

❹ Transfer the cake mixture to the prepared tin and bake in the preheated oven for 45 minutes. Check after

30 minutes and if it is browning too much, cover it with greaseproof paper or foil, or move it to a lower shelf. When the cake is cooked, turn out on to a cake rack and allow to cool. Dust the cake with a little icing sugar, for a 'snow' effect.

Tony Hogger
Blackshots, Grays

Preparation Time: 20 minutes
Cooking Time: 45 minutes
Oven Temperature: 190°C/375°F/Gas Mark 5

Reader's Tip: A smooth marmalade is probably your best choice for this cake.

Swiss Roll

125 g/4 oz caster sugar, plus
  a little extra for dusting
3 eggs
65 g/2$^1/_2$ oz plain flour, sifted
$^1/_4$ teaspoon salt
warm jam and whipped
  cream, for filling

❶ Preheat the oven to 190°C/375°F/Gas Mark 5. Put the caster sugar on aluminium foil on a heat-resistant plate in the centre of the oven for 6 minutes.

❷ Meanwhile, grease a Swiss roll tin and oil a sheet of greaseproof paper cut to the size of the tin.

❸ Beat the eggs for 10 minutes and add the sugar. Then gently fold in the flour and salt with a spatula.

❹ Spread the mixture evenly into the prepared tin and cook in the preheated oven for 12–15 minutes until golden brown, well risen and springy to the touch.

5 Meanwhile, have ready a sheet of greaseproof paper heavily dusted with caster sugar over a folded newspaper. Run a knife around the edges of the cake, turn it out on to the prepared greaseproof paper. Leave to cool and, after about 30–45 minutes, spread the surface with warmed jam and cream. Roll up with the aid of the paper.

Daphne King-Brewster
Holyhead, North Wales

Preparation Time:	30 minutes, plus cooling time
Cooking Time:	12–15 minutes
Oven Temperature:	190°C/375°F/Gas Mark 5
Reader's Tip:	Choose a good-quality jam for the filling, with a high percentage of fruit.

APPLE CAKE

250 g/8 oz self-raising flour
125 g/4 oz butter or mar-
  garine
125 g/4 oz soft light brown
  sugar
250 g/8 oz peeled and
  roughly diced cooking
  apple

1 medium egg
1 tablespoon milk
2 tablespoons caster sugar
$1/2$ teaspoon cinnamon

❶ Grease and flour a rectangular baking tin about 28 x 18 cm/11 x 7 inches. Preheat the oven to 200°C/400°F/ Gas Mark 6.

❷ Sieve the flour into a mixing bowl and rub in the butter or margarine with your fingertips until the mixture resembles fine breadcrumbs.

❸ Stir in the brown sugar and cooking apple, then add the egg and the milk to make a fairly stiff mixture, with a reluctant dropping consistency.

❹ Mix together the caster sugar and cinnamon, and set aside. Put the cake mixture into the prepared cake tin and sprinkle the reserved mixture of sugar and cinnamon over the top of the cake.

5 Bake in the preheated oven for 30–35 minutes. Turn out and allow to cool on a cake rack, and cut into squares to serve.

Tony Hogger
Blackshots, Grays

'Bramleys are the best choice of apple for this cake – no question. When they are cooked, they become mouthwateringly fluffy inside.'

Makes 16 x 5 cm/2 inch squares

Preparation Time: 20 minutes
Cooking Time: 30–35 minutes
Oven Temperature: 200°C/400°F/Gas Mark 6

Reader's Tip: It is best not to slice this cake until it is completely cool, otherwise it has a tendency to fall apart.

LEMON DRIZZLE CAKE

125 g/4 oz hard margarine,
  softened
75 g/3 oz sugar
2 eggs
150 g/5 oz self-raising flour
2 tablespoons lemon curd
grated rind of $\frac{1}{2}$ large lemon

Syrup
2 tablespoons granulated
  sugar
juice of 1 lemon

1 Grease and line a 1 kg/2 lb loaf tin and preheat the oven to 180°C/350°F/Gas Mark 4.

2 Cream together the margarine and sugar until soft. Then add a little of the egg and a little flour alternately. Add the lemon curd and rind.

3 Turn out the cake mixture into the prepared loaf tin and bake for 45 minutes–1 hour.

4 Meanwhile, to make the syrup, heat the sugar gently until dissolved, then add the lemon juice. Take off the heat and allow to cool.

⑤ When the cake is cooked, take it out of the oven but leave in the tin. Pour over the syrup and leave to cool.

Mrs. N. Ashworth
Lincoln

Preparation Time:	20 minutes
Cooking Time:	45 minutes–1 hour
Oven Temperature:	180°C/350°F/Gas Mark 4
Reader's Tip:	If the mixture curdles, add a little more flour while mixing in the egg.

Victoria Sponge

175 g/6 oz caster sugar

175 g/6 oz butter at room
temperature

3 large eggs at room temperature, beaten

3 drops vanilla essence

175 g/6 oz self-raising flour,
sifted

1$\frac{1}{2}$ teaspoons baking powder (optional)

a little milk

caster sugar, for dredging

❶ Grease and line two 18 cm/7 inch cake tins and preheat
the oven to 190°C/375°F/Gas Mark 5.

❷ Cream together the sugar and butter until pale and
fluffy. Add the eggs, a little at a time, beating well after
each addition, then add the vanilla essence. Fold in half
the flour and the baking powder, if using, with a metal
spoon, then fold in all the remaining flour and add a few
drops of milk to give it a dropping consistency.

❸ Place half the mixture in each cake tin and level it with
a palette knife. Bake both cakes on the middle shelf of
the preheated oven for about 20 minutes, turning the
tins halfway through the cooking time, or until well

risen, golden brown, firm to the touch and beginning to shrink away from the sides of the tins. Turn out and cool on a wire rack.

❹ When the cakes are cool, sandwich them together with cream, jam or butter cream, as you wish, and dredge with caster sugar.

John Wright
Grantown on Spey

'This is the definitive sponge mix, which was passed down from Mr. Wright's grandfather who was a master baker.'

Preparation Time:	20 minutes
Cooking Time:	about 20 minutes
Oven Temperature:	190°C/375°F/Gas Mark 5
Reader's Tip:	Do not use eggs straight from the fridge but take them out at least 30 minutes beforehand.

VICTORIA CAKE

125 g/4 oz butter, softened
4¹/₂ tablespoons caster sugar
2 large eggs
4¹/₂ tablespoons self-raising
  flour, sifted
1 teaspoon water or lemon
  juice

❶ Grease a 15–20 cm/6–8 inch Pyrex casserole dish, which will not stick as easily as a metal cake tin. Preheat the oven to 160°C/325°F/Gas Mark 3.

❷ Put the butter in a mixing bowl and then rub in the sugar using your fingers.

❸ Break in 1 of the eggs and mix in. Spoon in 1 tablespoon flour and mix in, then add the other egg and another tablespoon flour. Mix in the water or lemon juice, then tip in the remaining flour and mix this in.

❹ Transfer the cake mixture to the prepared casserole dish and bake in the preheated oven for 1¹/₄ hours. Then turn off the oven and leave the cake in the oven for another 15 minutes.

⑤ Allow the cake to cool, then run a knife blade around the dish and invert the cake.

Vera Hopwood
Craven Arms, Shropshire

Preparation Time:	20 minutes
Cooking Time:	1¼ hours
Oven Temperature:	160°C/325°F/Gas Mark 3
Reader's Tip:	A good way of softening the butter is to slice it and leave it in a plastic mixing bowl for a couple of hours at (warm) room temperature.

BUTTERING CAKE

125 g/4 oz margarine

125 g/4 oz sugar

250 ml/8 fl oz milk

250 g/8 oz dried fruit

250 g/8 oz self-raising flour,
   sifted

a pinch of salt

$1/4$ teaspoon ground
   cinnamon (optional)

1 egg, lightly beaten

❶ Grease and line a 1 kg/2 lb loaf tin and preheat the oven to 160°C/325°F/Gas Mark 3.

❷ Place the margarine, sugar, milk and fruit in a saucepan and heat gently until the sugar is dissolved. Leave to cool for 5 minutes.

❸ Add the flour, salt and cinnamon, if using. Mix well. Then add the egg and mix everything together with a wooden spoon.

❹ Turn out the cake mixture into the prepared loaf tin, then bake in the preheated oven for $1^{1}/_{4}$ hours. Leave to cool before turning it out, then slice before serving.

Vera Beba
Spalding

Preparation Time:	20 minutes
Cooking Time:	$1^{1}/_{4}$ hours
Oven Temperature:	160°C/325°F/Gas Mark 3
Reader's Tip:	Butter the slices of cake before eating them, and enjoy!

YOGURT CAKE

250 g/8 oz self-raising flour	50 ml/2 fl oz oil
125 g/4 oz sugar	125 g/4 oz plain yogurt
1 egg	
a few drops vanilla essence	

1 Grease and line a 1 kg/2 lb loaf tin and preheat the oven to 180°C/350°F/Gas Mark 4.

2 Combine the flour with the sugar, then beat in the egg, vanilla essence, oil and yogurt.

3 Pour the cake mixture into the prepared loaf tin and bake in the preheated oven for 1 hour. Turn out on to a cooling rack.

M. Atkinson
Wetherby

Preparation Time:	10 minutes
Cooking Time:	1 hour
Oven Temperature:	180°C/350°F/Gas Mark 4
Reader's Tip:	This yogurt cake is especially good when it is spread with a little of your favourite jam.

CINNAMON CAKE

250 g/8 oz plain flour
2 teaspoons baking powder
a pinch of salt
1 teaspoon cinnamon
125 g/4 oz butter or mar-
  garine
175 g/6 oz caster sugar
2 eggs, separated
150 ml/¹/₄ pint milk

Topping
1 tablespoon melted butter
¹/₂ teaspoon cinnamon
50 g/2 oz caster sugar
25 g/1 oz cornflakes

❶ Grease a 23 cm/9 inch cake tin. Preheat the oven to 190°C/375°F/Gas Mark 5.

❷ Sift together the flour, baking powder, salt and cinnamon into a large mixing bowl.

❸ Add the butter or margarine, sugar and egg yolks, and mix together well.

❹ Add the milk and stir until combined.

❺ Beat the egg whites until stiff and then fold into the cake mixture.

❻ Transfer the mixture to the prepared cake tin.

7 To make the topping, melt the butter and stir in the cinnamon, sugar and cornflakes. Scatter over the top of the cake.

8 Bake for about 30–35 minutes until cooked.

Moira Bourke
Glasgow

'It was an inspired idea to use cornflakes in the topping – they give a deliciously crunchy texture.'

Preparation Time:	25 minutes
Cooking Time:	30–35 minutes
Oven Temperature:	190°C/375°F/Gas Mark 5
Reader's Tip:	Use either the 'old-fashioned' (imperial) measures or the new (metric) ones as you prefer, but never mix the two.

WARTIME GINGERBREAD

250 g/8 oz sugar
250 ml/8 fl oz water
175 g/6 oz dried fruit
2 tablespoons black treacle
75 g/3 oz margarine
a few pieces of ginger in
   syrup, chopped, plus a little
   of the syrup
50 g/2 oz almonds, chopped
150 g/5 oz flour, sifted
1 teaspoon cinnamon
1 teaspoon ginger

1 teaspoon allspice
1 teaspoon baking powder
$1/2$ teaspoon bicarbonate of
   soda

❶ Grease and line a 1 kg/2 lb loaf tin. Preheat the oven to
180°C/350°F/Gas Mark 4.

❷ Put the sugar, water, dried fruit, black treacle, margarine,
ginger, syrup and chopped almonds in a saucepan, and
bring to the boil. Boil for 3 minutes, then allow to cool.
When the mixture is cold, stir and add the flour, cinnamon, ginger, allspice, baking powder and bicarbonate of
soda dissolved in a little hot water. Mix well.

❸ Transfer the cake mixture to the prepared loaf tin and bake in the preheated oven for 1 hour.

Sarah Innes
Colinsburgh Leven, Fife

Preparation Time:	20 minutes, plus cooling time
Cooking Time:	1 hour
Oven Temperature:	180°C/350°F/Gas Mark 4
Reader's Tip:	This was given to me by my 90-year-old sister-in-law. It has no eggs, which were rationed during the war.

All-in-One Sponge

175 g/6 oz self-raising flour,
  sifted
1 teaspoon baking powder
175 g/6 oz soft margarine
175 g/6 oz caster sugar
2 large eggs
2–3 drops vanilla essence

❶ Grease and line two 18 cm/7 inch cake tins, no less than 2.5 cm/1 inch deep. Preheat the oven to 160°C/325°F/Gas Mark 3.

❷ Combine all the ingredients in a mixing bowl and whisk with an electric hand whisk for 1 minute, or until everything is thoroughly mixed.

❸ Divide the mixture between the two prepared cake tins, level off the cake mixture with a knife and bake on the centre shelf of the preheated oven for about 35 minutes, or until the cakes are coming away from the sides of the tins and the centre springs back when gently pressed with a finger.

❹ When the cakes are cooked, leave them in the tins for about 30 seconds before turning them out on to a cake rack to cool.

5 When the cakes are cool, sandwich them together with jam or sliced strawberries and whipped cream.

Jill M. White
Tavistock, Devon

'This is quick and easy to make and looks most impressive at a summer tea party.'

Preparation Time: 10 minutes
Cooking Time: 35 minutes
Oven Temperature: 160°C/325°F/Gas Mark 3

Reader's Tip: This cake is easy to adapt into a chocolate cake by omitting the vanilla and adding 2 tablespoons of sifted cocoa and 1 tablespoon of milk. When the cakes are cool, sandwich them together with 150 g/5 oz of good-quality plain chocolate mixed with 150 ml/5 fl oz of soured cream. Decorate the top of the cake with the same mixture.

Banana Bread

125 g/4 oz butter	75 g/3 oz walnuts, coarsely
150 g/5 oz caster sugar	chopped
2 large eggs	250 g/8 oz self-raising flour,
3 bananas	sifted
	$1/_2$ teaspoon salt

❶ Line a 23 cm/9 inch loaf tin with greaseproof paper. Brush with melted butter and set aside. Preheat the oven to 180°C/350°F/Gas Mark 4.

❷ Cream together the butter and sugar until fluffy, then beat in the eggs.

❸ Peel and mash the bananas with a fork and add them to the mixture, together with the walnuts. Fold in the flour and salt.

❹ Spoon the mixture into the prepared loaf tin and bake in the preheated oven for 1 hour.

❺ When the cake is cooked, turn it out on a wire rack and allow to cool.

Moira Bourke
Glasgow

Preparation Time:	25 minutes
Cooking Time:	1 hour
Oven Temperature:	180°C/350°F/Gas Mark 4
Reader's Tip:	If you have a fan-assisted oven, you should reduce the cooking time by about 5–7 minutes.

AMERICAN POUND CAKE

375 g/12 oz butter   **1¹/₂ teaspoons vanilla essence**
250 g/8 oz cream cheese   **6 eggs**
700 g/23 oz sugar   **375 g/12 oz plain flour, sifted**
a pinch of salt

❶ Grease a ring cake tin and preheat the oven to 160°C/325°F/Gas Mark 3.

❷ Put the butter and cream cheese in a food processor and mix until pale and creamy.

❸ Add the sugar, salt and vanilla essence, and mix until very pale and creamy.

❹ Add the eggs 1 at a time, mixing thoroughly after each addition. Pour into a large mixing bowl, and fold in the flour.

❺ Bake in the prepared ring cake tin in the preheated oven for 1–1¹/₂ hours.

Rachel Perry
East Molesey, Surrey

Preparation Time:	15 minutes
Cooking Time:	1–1¹/₂ hours
Oven Temperature:	160°C/325°F/Gas Mark 3
Reader's Tip:	To test that the cake is cooked, insert a skewer. If it comes out clean, the cake is done.

ORANGE CAKE

125 g/4 oz soft margarine
125 g/4 oz caster sugar
75 g/3 oz self-raising flour,
  sifted
2 eggs, beaten
4 tablespoons milk
grated rind of 1 orange

Orange syrup
juice of 1 orange
50 g/2 oz caster sugar

❶ Grease and line an 18 cm/7 inch cake tin. Preheat the oven to 180°C/350°F/Gas Mark 4.

❷ Cream together the margarine and sugar in a mixing bowl. Gradually mix in the flour, eggs, milk and orange rind until you have a fairly smooth mixture.

❸ Put the cake mixture in the prepared cake tin and bake in the preheated oven for about 30 minutes, until the cake is coming away from the sides of the tin and the centre springs back when gently pressed with a finger.

❹ Meanwhile, make the orange syrup. Heat the orange juice and caster sugar in a saucepan over a low heat until the sugar is dissolved.

⑤ When the cake is cooked, leave it in the tin and prick over the surface with the prongs of a fork or a knitting needle. Pour the syrup carefully over the cake and leave until quite cold.

Mrs J. T. Kenner
Taunton, Somerset

'This is a lovely alternative to lemon cake - still with a strong citrus flavour but not quite so tangy.'

Preparation Time:	20 minutes
Cooking Time:	about 30 minutes
Oven Temperature:	180°C/350°F/Gas Mark 4
Reader's Tip:	Check whether the cake is cooked after 25 minutes in case your oven cooks more quickly – ovens vary a lot. If it is not ready, return the cake to the oven and cook for another 5 minutes or so.

BANANA AND HONEY TEABREAD

125 g/4 oz butter or mar-
  garine
50 g/2 oz soft brown sugar
2 tablespoons clear honey
2 eggs, beaten

175 g/6 oz self-raising flour
2 large ripe bananas
1 teaspoon ground mixed
  spice

❶ Grease and line a 1 kg/2 lb loaf tin with greaseproof paper, then grease the paper. Preheat the oven to 180°C/350°F/Gas Mark 4.

❷ Cream together the butter or margarine, sugar and honey, until the mixture is light and fluffy.

❸ Beat in the eggs, a little at a time, adding 1 tablespoon of flour after each addition of egg.

❹ Peel and mash the bananas. Stir the mashed bananas into the creamed mixture. Sift together the remaining flour and mixed spice, and fold carefully into the creamed mixture until evenly incorporated.

❺ Pour into the prepared loaf tin, level the surface and bake in the preheated oven for $1^{1}/_{4}$–$1^{1}/_{2}$ hours until firm to the touch.

6 Leave to cool in the tin for 1 minute, then turn out on to a wire rack and carefully peel off the lining paper. Turn the cake right way up, and leave to cool completely. Serve sliced, spread with butter if liked.

Gloria Cann
White Waltham, Berkshire

'This teabread is an ideal way of using up over-ripe, discoloured bananas. It's also delicious.'

Preparation Time:	25 minutes
Cooking Time:	1¹/₄–1¹/₂ hours
Oven Temperature:	180°C/350°F/Gas Mark 4
Reader's Tip:	The cooked teabread freezes particularly well. Simply wrap it up in a polythene bag, seal, label and freeze for up to 2 months. To thaw, unwrap the teabread and leave it to stand at room temperature for 4 hours. It will keep beautifully moist and fresh for up to 4 or 5 days after thawing.

Easy Apple Cake

500g/1 lb cooking apples
175 g/6 oz self-raising flour,
  sifted
1 teaspoon baking powder
175 g/6 oz caster sugar

2 eggs
$^1/_2$ teaspoon almond essence
125 g/4 oz butter, melted
caster sugar, to sprinkle

❶ Line a 20 cm/8 inch loose-bottom cake tin with greaseproof paper. Heat the oven to 180°C/350°F/Gas Mark 4.

❷ Peel, core and finely slice the apples and put them in a bowl of water.

❸ Put the flour and baking powder in a bowl with the caster sugar.

❹ Beat together the eggs and almond essence, and stir into the flour together with the melted butter. Mix together well.

❺ Spread half the mixture into the prepared cake tin.

❻ Drain and dry the apples on kitchen paper, and arrange on top of the cake mixture.

7 Top with the remaining cake mixture.

8 Bake the cake in the preheated oven for 1¹⁄₄ hours, or until the cake is golden brown. Then leave to cool for 15 minutes.

Ann Meddings
Kingston, Surrey

'I first tasted this yummy cake when I was a schoolgirl - now, at last, I have the recipe.'

Preparation Time:	15 minutes
Cooking Time:	1¹⁄₄ hours
Oven Temperature:	180C/350°F/Gas Mark 4
Reader's Tip:	You can buy a useful gadget that both cores and slices an apple in one operation from most good kitchen shops.

Seed Cake

175 g/6 oz soft margarine   **250 g/8 oz self-raising flour**
175 g/6 oz caster sugar   **1 teaspoon caraway seeds**
3 medium eggs

❶ Grease and line an 18 cm/7 inch cake tin. Preheat the oven to 160°C/325°F/Gas Mark 3.

❷ Place all the ingredients in a mixing bowl and mix together well. Place the cake mixture in the prepared cake tin and bake on the middle shelf of the preheated oven for 1$\frac{1}{2}$ hours.

❸ When the cake is cooked, turn out on to a cooling rack and allow to cool.

Ivy Jarvis
Framfield, Sussex

'Ivy is an old pal of my grandfather's and, after much coaxing, she parted with this no-fail cake.'

Preparation Time: 10 minutes
Cooking Time: 1$\frac{1}{2}$ hours
Oven Temperature: 160°C/325°F/Gas Mark 3

Reader's Tip: Caraway seeds, which have a distinctive
                             flavour, are a favourite ingredient in
                             central and northern Europe.

3
FRUIT CAKES

DATE CAKE

250 ml/8 fl oz boiling water
125–175 g/4–6 oz dates
50 g/2 oz butter
125 g/4 oz caster sugar
1 egg

250 g/8oz self-raising flour,
 sifted
1 teaspoon bicarbonate of
 soda

❶ Grease and line the base of a 1.2 litre/2 pint loaf tin and preheat the oven to 180°C/350°F/Gas Mark 4.

❷ Pour the boiling water over the dates in a bowl and leave for 20 minutes.

❸ Cream together the butter and sugar in a mixing bowl. Add the egg, flour and bicarbonate of soda to the dates (including the liquid), then add this mixture to the creamed butter and sugar.

❹ Place the mixture in the prepared loaf tin and bake in the preheated oven for about 1 hour until golden and firm to the touch. Turn out and cool on a wire rack.

E. Ridout
New Malden, Essex

Preparation Time:	15 minutes, plus 20 minutes soaking time
Cooking Time:	1 hour
Oven Temperature:	180°C/350°F/Gas Mark 4
Reader's Tip:	Soaking the dates in boiling water softens them and keeps them moist.

FRUIT TEABREAD

300 g/10 oz sultanas and
  raisins, mixed
200 g/7 oz soft brown sugar
300 ml/$\frac{1}{2}$ pint cold tea,
  strained

1 large egg
300 g/10 oz wholewheat
  flour

❶ Put the fruit and sugar in a large mixing bowl. Pour over the cold tea and leave overnight.

❷ The following day, grease and line a 1 kg/2 lb loaf tin, making sure that the lining paper is sufficiently high at the ends to enable you to take the cake out of the tin easily when it is cooked. Preheat the oven to 160°C/325°F/Gas Mark 3.

❸ Stir the mixture, add the egg and flour, and mix until smooth. Pour into the prepared tin and level the top of the mixture. Bake in the centre of the preheated oven for $1\frac{1}{4}$–$1\frac{1}{2}$ hours until a sharp skewer comes out clean.

Mrs M. West

Preparation Time:	10 minutes, plus overnight soaking time
Cooking Time:	$1\frac{1}{4}$–$1\frac{1}{2}$ hours
Oven Temperature:	160°C/325°F/Gas Mark 3
Reader's Tip:	Choose your favourite variety of tea to make this cake. If you like Earl Grey, for example, use that to soak the fruit and sugar.

ALL-IN-ONE FRUIT CAKE

250 g/8 oz self-raising flour	125 ml/4 fl oz milk
1 teaspoon mixed spice	125 g/4 oz caster sugar
125 g/4 oz soft margarine	375 g/12 oz mixed dried fruit
2 eggs	

1 Grease and line a 1 kg/2 lb loaf tin and preheat the oven to 160°C/325°F/Gas Mark 3.

2 Sift the flour and mixed spice together. Add all the remaining ingredients and beat them together for 2–3 minutes until thoroughly mixed.

3 Place the cake mixture in the prepared loaf tin and bake in the centre of the preheated oven for about $1^3/_4$ hours. Test with a knife – if it comes out clean, it is ready.

4 Allow the cake to cool in the tin for 10 minutes and then transfer to a cooling rack to cool completely.

Liz Kirkwood
Petts Wood, Kent

Preparation Time:	15 minutes
Cooking Time:	$1^3/_4$ hours
Oven Temperature:	160°C/325°F/Gas Mark 3
Reader's Tip:	This recipe leaves plenty of scope for variation. You can use any dried fruits that you like: sultanas, currants, raisins, glacé cherries, or any other dried fruits that take your fancy. You can also add almond or vanilla essence to the milk, as you prefer.

DATE AND GINGER SLAB

125 g/4 oz butter

125 g/4 oz soft brown sugar

50 g/2 oz golden syrup

50–75 g/2–3 oz chopped
   dates

2 large or 3 small eggs, beaten

175 g/6 oz self-raising flour,
   sifted

2 teaspoons ginger

2 teaspoons bicarbonate of
   soda

❶ Grease and line two 1 kg/2 lb loaf tins and preheat the oven to 160°C/325°F/Gas Mark 3.

❷ Melt the butter with the sugar, syrup and dates in a large saucepan. Leave to cool a little. Then add the eggs, flour, ginger and bicarbonate of soda, and mix well.

❸ Put the cake mixture in the prepared loaf tins and cook in the preheated oven for about 1–1¼ hours until cooked.

Mrs N. Ashworth
Lincoln

'The first time I made this cake, it sunk because I opened the door too often - a warning.'

Preparation Time: 15 minutes

Cooking Time: 1–1¼ hours

Oven Temperature: 160°C/325°F/Gas Mark 3

Reader's Tip: This cake freezes well once it is cooked.
     Spread with butter to serve.

CUT AND COME AGAIN CAKE

250 g/8 oz self-raising flour,
 sifted

¹/₄ teaspoon salt

1 teaspoon mixed spice

125 g/4 oz sugar

275 g/9 oz mixed dried fruit

1 teaspoon grated orange or
 lemon rind

125 g/4 oz soft margarine

150 ml/¹/₄ pint milk and
 water mixed

1 egg, beaten

❶ Grease and line a 15 cm/6 inch cake tin or a 1 kg/2 lb loaf tin, and preheat the oven to 180°C/350°F/Gas Mark 4.

❷ Mix together all the dry ingredients, then add the margarine, milk and water and the beaten egg. Turn out the mixture into the prepared cake or loaf tin.

❸ Bake in the preheated oven for 1 hour 15–20 minutes until well risen, golden brown, firm to the touch and beginning to shrink away from the sides of the tin.

Jenny Heughan
Theydon Bois, Essex

Preparation Time: 10 minutes
Cooking Time: 1 hour 15–20 minutes
Oven Temperature: 180°C/350°F/Gas Mark 4

Reader's Tip: The sugar in this recipe may be
                           brown or white, as you prefer.

Bara Brith

1 mug hot tea	2 mugs self-raising flour,
1 mug brown sugar	sifted
1 mug mixed dried fruit	1 egg

❶ Put the hot tea in a bowl, then add the sugar and dried fruit. Stir well to dissolve the sugar and leave to stand overnight.

❷ The following day, butter and line an oblong 500 g/1 lb cake tin and preheat the oven to 180°C/350°F/Gas Mark 4.

❸ Add the flour and egg to the bowl. Beat well and turn into the prepared cake tin. Bake in the preheated oven for 45–50 minutes, or until a skewer inserted into the centre of the cake comes out clean.

❹ Turn out on to a cooling rack and allow to cool.

Barbara Steele
Swansea, Wales

Preparation Time:	15 minutes, plus overnight standing time
Cooking Time:	45–50 minutes
Oven Temperature:	180°C/350°F/Gas Mark 4
Reader's Tip:	Cut this cake into thin slices and butter. Just delicious!

MARMALADE FRUIT CAKE

125 g/4 oz soft margarine

125 g/4 oz soft light brown
sugar

375 g/12 oz mixed fruit

1 tablespoon marmalade

250 ml/8 fl oz warm water

250 g/8 oz self-raising flour

$1/2$ teaspoon bicarbonate of
soda

1 teaspoon mixed spice

2 eggs, lightly beaten

1 Lightly grease and line a 20 cm/8 inch cake tin and preheat the oven to 160°C/325°F/Gas Mark 3.

2 Place the soft margarine, soft brown sugar, mixed fruit, marmalade and warm water in a saucepan and bring gently to a simmer over low heat. Simmer for just 3 minutes, then allow to cool.

3 Sift together the remaining dry ingredients (the self-raising flour, the bicarbonate of soda and the mixed spice) into a large mixing bowl.

4 Now add the cooled fruit mixture to the flour, then add the eggs and mix together thoroughly.

5 Pour the cake mixture into the prepared cake tin and bake in the preheated oven for about 1 hour–1 hour 10 minutes.

6 Leave in the tin to cool, then turn out on to a wire rack
and leave until completely cold.

Gwen Stevenson
Haywards Heath, East Sussex

'If you're fond of marmalade,
you'll just love this cake. I find
home-made marmalade tastes better.'

Preparation Time:	20 minutes, plus cooling time
Cooking Time:	1 hour–1 hour 10 minutes
Oven Temperature:	160°C/325°F/Gas Mark 3
Reader's Tip:	The marmalade adds something special to this cake. Use orange, lemon or lime marmalade – even ginger marmalade – as you wish. You can, of course, omit it completely if you don't like marmalade, though you'll also have to change the name of the cake.

TEA LOAF

375 g/12 oz dried mixed fruit   300 g/10 oz self-raising flour
175 g/6 oz soft brown sugar   1 teaspoon mixed spice
a little tea (enough to cover   1 teaspoon cinnamon
   the fruit)   1 egg, beaten

❶ Soak the dried fruit and sugar overnight in the tea.

❷ The following day, stir in the flour, mixed spice, cinnamon and beaten egg.

❸ Grease and line two 500 g/1 lb loaf tins and preheat the oven to 180°C/350°F/Gas Mark 4.

❹ Divide the mixture into the two prepared loaf tins and bake in the preheated oven for about 45 minutes. Turn out on to a cooling rack and cool.

❺ Slice and eat, with or without butter, as preferred.

Norah Hinde
Redcar, Cleveland

Preparation Time:	15 minutes, plus overnight soaking time
Cooking Time:	45 minutes
Oven Temperature:	180°C/350°F/Gas Mark 4
Reader's Tip:	The beauty of this cake recipe – quite apart from the fact that it is absolutely delicious – is that it is totally fat free.

LIGHT FRUIT CAKE

150 g/5 oz butter or margarine	250 g/8 oz currants
125 g/4 oz caster sugar	250 g/8 oz raisins
3 eggs	125 g/4 oz cherries
250 g/8 oz self-raising flour	75 g/3 oz ground almonds
	1 tablespoon milk

❶ Grease and line a 20 cm/8 inch round cake tin. Preheat the oven to 160°C/325°F/Gas Mark 3.

❷ Cream together the butter or margarine and sugar, then add the eggs, flour, fruit, almonds and milk, and mix well.

❸ Turn out the cake mixture into the prepared cake tin and bake in the preheated oven for about 2 hours or until the cake springs back when pressed in the centre.

Mrs J. V. Moss
Whitehaven, Cumbria

Preparation Time:	20 minutes
Cooking Time:	2 hours
Oven Temperature:	160°C/325°F/Gas Mark 3
Reader's Tip:	This cake takes very little time to prepare and a long time to cook. It is well worth it.

Farmhouse Fruit Cake

125 g/4 oz plain flour
a pinch of salt
125 g/4 oz wholewheat flour
2 teaspoons baking powder
1 teaspoon mixed spice
$^1/_2$ teaspoon ground
cinnamon
125 g/4 oz soft brown sugar

125 g/4 oz butter or
margarine
250 g/8 oz mixed dried fruit
50 g/2 oz chopped mixed
peel
3 eggs, beaten
2 tablespoons marmalade
2 tablespoons milk (optional)

❶ Grease and line a 20 cm/8 inch round cake tin with greased greaseproof paper. Preheat the oven to 160°C/325°F/Gas Mark 3.

❷ Sift the flour and salt into a mixing bowl, then stir in the wholewheat flour, baking powder, mixed spice, cinnamon and sugar.

❸ Rub in the butter or margarine. Stir in the remaining ingredients and mix well. Stir in a little milk if the mixture seems too stiff. The cake mixture should be of a reluctant dropping consistency.

❹ Spoon into the prepared cake tin and bake in the preheated oven for about 1–1$^1/_4$ hours or until a skewer inserted in the centre comes out clean. Cover the top of the cake with greaseproof paper if the cake begins to become too brown during the cooking.

5 Remove from the oven, take out of the tin and discard the greaseproof paper. Cool on a wire rack and store in an airtight tin.

Diane Lawton
Marlow Bottom, Buckinghamshire

'This is a deliciously wholesome fruit cake.'

Preparation Time:	15 minutes
Cooking Time:	1–1¼ hours
Oven Temperature:	160°C/325°F/Gas Mark 3
Reader's Tip:	Farmhouse fruit cake is a country recipe using wholewheat flour, which is – as you know – much better for you. It keeps well and even improves with age – if given the chance.

FRUITY GINGERBREAD

125 g/4 oz butter
125 g/4 oz soft brown sugar
125 g/4 oz black treacle
1 egg, beaten
125 g/4 oz plain flour
2 teaspoons ground ginger
2 teaspoons ground
  cinnamon

125 g/4 oz wholewheat flour
about 150 ml/$^1/_4$ pint warm
  milk
1 teaspoon bicarbonate of
  soda
50 g/2 oz mixed dried fruit

❶ Grease and line a rectangular 23 x 15 cm/9 x 6 inch
cake tin or a 20 cm/8 inch round cake tin with greaseproof paper. Preheat the oven to 150°C/300°F/Gas
Mark 2.

❷ Put the butter, sugar and treacle in a saucepan and heat
gently over low heat until melted, stirring constantly.
Allow to cool slightly, then beat in the egg.

❸ Sift the plain flour and spices into a mixing bowl, then
stir in the wholewheat flour and melted butter mixture,
and beat well to combine.

❹ Mix the milk with the bicarbonate of soda and add this
to the mixture in the bowl. Stir in the fruit. The mixture should have a soft dropping consistency. If it seems
too dry, add a little more milk.

5 Spoon the mixture into the prepared cake tin. Bake in the preheated oven for about 1 hour 10 minutes, or until a skewer inserted in the centre comes out clean.

6 Leave the cake to cool in the tin, then remove the cake from the tin and discard the greaseproof paper.

Diane Lawton
Marlow Bottom, Buckinghamshire

'Prunes and dried apricots can be used instead of dates in this recipe.'

Preparation Time:	25 minutes
Cooking Time:	1 hour 10 minutes
Oven Temperature:	150°C/300°F/Gas Mark 2
Reader's Tip:	Gingerbread always improves and becomes moist and soft if it is kept for a while before eating. When it is cold, place it in an airtight tin and leave for about a week. Then cut into squares.

DATE AND WALNUT LOAF

250 g/8 oz stoned dates,
 chopped
1 teaspoon bicarbonate of
 soda
a pinch of salt
300 ml/^{1}/$_2$ pint hot water
300 g/10 oz self-raising flour
125 g/4 oz butter or
 margarine, cut in pieces
50 g/2 oz shelled walnuts,
 chopped
125 g/4 oz dark soft brown
 sugar
1 egg, beaten

❶ Grease a 1 kg/2 lb loaf tin. Preheat the oven to 180°C/350°F/Gas Mark 4.

❷ Put the dates, bicarbonate of soda and salt in a mixing bowl and pour over the hot water. Set aside until cool.

❸ Meanwhile, sift the flour into a mixing bowl. Add the butter or margarine and rub into the flour. Stir in the walnuts and sugar until thoroughly combined.

4 Mix the dry ingredients into the cooled date mixture and beat in the egg. Pour into the prepared loaf tin and bake in the preheated oven for 1–1¼ hours or until a skewer inserted in the centre comes out clean. Turn out on to a wire cooling rack and leave to cool.

Diane Lawton
Marlow Bottom, Buckinghamshire

'*Prunes and dried apricots can be used instead of dates in this recipe.*'

Preparation Time:	15 minutes, plus cooling time
Cooking Time:	1–1¼ hours
Oven Temperature:	180°C/350°F/Gas Mark 4
Reader's Tip:	This makes the perfect teatime treat. It actually improves with age as long as it is kept in an airtight tin.

CIDER CAKE

375 g/12 oz mixed dried fruit
175 g/6 oz soft dark sugar
300 ml/$^1/_2$ pint medium
  sweet cider
1 large egg, beaten
50 g/2 oz butter, melted
375 g/12 oz self-raising flour,
  sifted

❶ Soak the dried fruit and sugar in the cider overnight.

❷ The following day, grease and line a 1 kg/2 lb loaf tin with baking parchment. Preheat the oven to 190°C/375°F/Gas Mark 5.

❸ Add the beaten egg and melted butter to the fruit mixture. Fold in the flour. At this stage, the mixture should be quite soft.

❹ Spoon the mixture into the prepared loaf tin and bake in the preheated oven for 1 hour–1 hour 20 minutes. Test with a wooden skewer after 1 hour, and if the skewer is clean on withdrawal, the cake is cooked.

⑤ Cool the cake on a cake rack. This cake is best after a couple of days' storage in a cake tin with a well-fitting lid. Do not use a plastic cake box. It freezes well, too. Serve sliced, plain or spread with butter.

Jill M. White
Tavistock, Devon

Preparation Time:	15 minutes, plus overnight soaking
Cooking Time:	1 hour–1 hour 20 minutes
Oven Temperature:	190°C/375°F/Gas Mark 5
Reader's Tip:	If this cake is browning too much during the cooking process, cover it with aluminium foil.

Vinegar Fruit Cake

175 g/6 oz butter or
  margarine
375 g/12 oz self-raising flour
175 g/6 oz sugar
250 g/8 oz sultanas

1 teaspoon mixed spice
  (optional)
1 teaspoon bicarbonate of
  soda
2 tablespoons vinegar
300 ml/½ pint milk

❶ Grease and flour a 20 cm/8 inch cake tin. Preheat the oven to 190°C/375°F/Gas Mark 5.

❷ Mix together the fat and flour, then add the sugar, sultanas and mixed spice, if using.

❸ Stir the bicarbonate of soda and vinegar into the milk and add this mixture to all the other ingredients.

❹ Pour the cake mixture into the prepared cake tin. Bake in the preheated oven for about 1½ hours, or until a skewer or metal knitting needle inserted into the centre of the cake comes out clean.

Rosemary Cowan
Penzance, Cornwall

Preparation Time:	15 minutes
Cooking Time:	1½ hours
Oven Temperature:	190°C/375°F/Gas Mark 5
Reader's Tip:	Vinegar might seem like a strange addition, but fear not – it's actually remarkably good.

MINCEMEAT FRUIT CAKE

250 g/8 oz self-raising flour
3 eggs
500 g/1 lb mincemeat
150 g/5 oz caster sugar or
   soft brown sugar

150 g/5 oz soft margarine
75 g/3 oz sultanas
25 g/1 oz flaked almonds
   (optional)

❶ Grease and line a 20 cm/8 inch cake tin with grease-proof paper, and grease again. Preheat the oven to 160°C/325°F/Gas Mark 3.

❷ Place all the ingredients, except the almonds, in a bowl and beat together well for about 1 minute.

❸ Put the cake mixture into the tin, sprinkle the flaked almonds on the top, if liked, and bake in the preheated oven for $1^3/_4$ hours. When the cake is cooked, the sides will shrink away from the tin and a skewer put into the middle of the cake should come out clean. Leave the cake in the tin for a few minutes and then allow to cool completely on a cake rack.

Phillip D. Pearson
Kingswinford, West Midlands

Preparation Time:	10 minutes
Cooking Time:	$1^3/_4$ hours
Oven Temperature:	160°C/325°F/Gas Mark 3
Reader's Tip:	If any children are likely to be eating this cake, do not use the almonds in case of nut allergies.

BOILED FRUIT CAKE

250 g/8 oz mixed dried fruit
a few chopped glacé cherries
125 g/4 oz margarine
175 g/6 oz self-raising flour
1 teaspoon mixed spice
175 g/6 oz sugar
2 eggs, beaten
a little demerara sugar, for
  sprinkling

❶ Grease and line a 1 kg/2 lb loaf tin. Preheat the oven to 180°C/350°F/Gas Mark 4.

❷ Put the fruit into a saucepan, cover with water and boil for 5 minutes, then remove from the heat. Drain off the water and add all the remaining ingredients, except for the demerara sugar, to the pan and mix well.

❸ Pour the cake mixture into the prepared loaf tin. Sprinkle the demerara sugar on top. Bake in the pre-heated oven for 30 minutes, and then lower the oven temperature to 160°C/325°F/Gas Mark 3 and bake for a further 45 minutes.

❹ When the cake is cooked, leave it in the tin for about 5 minutes and then turn out on to a cake rack to cool.

Pamela Stevens
Pangbourne, Berkshire

Preparation Time:	20 minutes
Cooking Time:	1¼ hours
Oven Temperature:	180°C/350°F/Gas Mark 4, then 160°C/325°F/Gas Mark 3
Reader's Tip:	This cake can equally well be cooked in an 18 cm/7 inch round cake tin.

CHRISTMAS CAKE

500 g/1 lb butter
250 g/8 oz plain flour, sifted
250 g/8 oz self-raising flour,
  sifted
375 g/12 oz soft brown
  sugar
1 teaspoon mixed spice
500 g/1 lb mixed dried fruit
1 teaspoon almond essence
1 teaspoon vanilla essence
6 eggs, beaten
demerara sugar, to sprinkle

❶ Grease and line a 20 cm/8 inch deep-sided square cake
tin with 3–4 sheets of greaseproof paper and baking
parchment. Preheat the oven to 150°C/300°F/Gas
Mark 2.

❷ Rub the butter into the flour, and add the sugar, mixed
spice, dried fruit, and the almond and vanilla essences.
Then add the eggs and mix well. Spoon the mixture
into the prepared tin. Sprinkle with demerara sugar.

❸ Bake in the preheated oven for $2^1/_2$–3 hours. Check after 2 hours, pushing a skewer into the middle of the cake. If it isn't cooked, put it back in the oven and check every 30 minutes until the skewer comes out clean.

Patricia Stockham
Honiton, Devon

Preparation Time:	30 minutes
Cooking Time:	$2^1/_2$–3 hours
Oven Temperature:	150°C/300°F/Gas Mark 2
Reader's Tip:	Don't overfill the tin – better to use two than to overfill one. Make this a few weeks before Christmas and brush it with brandy every few nights.

Guggy Fruit Cake

200 g/7 oz soft light brown
  sugar
175 g/6 oz sultanas
175 g/6 oz currants
250 ml/8 fl oz water

125 g/4 oz margarine
2 teaspoons mixed spice
300 g/10 oz self-raising flour,
  sifted

1 Grease and line a 20 cm/8 inch round, deep-sided cake tin and preheat the oven to 180°C/350°F/Gas Mark 4.

2 Put the sugar, dried fruit, water, margarine and mixed spice in a saucepan and heat gently to melt the margarine into the mixture. Leave to cool, then stir in the flour.

3 Transfer the cake mixture to the prepared cake tin and bake in the preheated oven for about 1 hour.

4 When the cake is cooked, turn it out on to a cake rack and allow to cool.

Anon

Preparation Time:	20 minutes
Cooking Time:	1 hour
Oven Temperature:	180°C/350°F/Gas Mark 4
Reader's Tip:	It is not necessary to slave for hours to produce wholesome and good-looking cakes. This recipe is simple and easy, and very quick to make.

JENNY CAKE

125 g/4 oz granulated sugar
250 g/8 oz self-raising flour
375 g/12 oz mixed fruit
125 g/4 oz margarine,
  melted

4 medium eggs, beaten
150 ml/¼ pint milk
a pinch of nutmeg
1 teaspoon mixed spice

❶ Grease and line a deep 18 cm/7 inch cake tin. Preheat the oven to 150°C/300°F/Gas Mark 2.

❷ Put the sugar, flour and mixed fruit in a food processor and mix. Then add the margarine and eggs, and mix well. Add the cold milk and then the nutmeg and mixed spice.

❸ Pour the cake mixture into the prepared cake tin and bake in the centre of the preheated oven for 2 hours 10 minutes.

❹ Remove the cake from the oven and leave in the tin for about 30 minutes to cool slightly before turning out on to a cooling rack.

Eileen and Jenny
Wednesfield, Wolverhampton

Preparation Time:	20 minutes
Cooking Time:	2 hours 10 minutes
Oven Temperature:	150°C/300°F/Gas Mark 2
Reader's Tip:	Use as much nutmeg as you like. We tend to use a big pinch.

Mrs. Atherton's Loaf

65 ml/2^1/$_2$ fl oz water

250 g/8 oz mixed dried fruit

25 g/1 oz chopped nuts

65 g/2^1/$_2$ oz margarine

1 dessertspoon marmalade

50 g/2 oz soft brown sugar

^{1}/$_2$ teaspoon ground ginger

^{1}/$_2$ teaspoon mixed spice

1 egg

65 ml/2^1/$_2$ fl oz milk

^{1}/$_2$ teaspoon bicarbonate of soda

175 g/6 oz self-raising flour, sifted

❶ Grease and line a 500 g/1 lb loaf tin. Preheat the oven to 180°C/350°F/Gas Mark 4.

❷ Put the water, mixed dried fruit, chopped nuts, margarine, marmalade, soft brown sugar, ground ginger and mixed spice in a saucepan. Heat gently over a low heat and bring to the boil.

❸ Remove the pan from the heat and then allow to stand for 2 minutes only. Now beat together until all the ingredients are mixed together well.

❹ Stir in the egg, milk and bicarbonate of soda, and then stir in the flour.

⑤ Put the cake mixture in the prepared loaf tin and bake just above the centre of the preheated oven for about 45 minutes.

⑥ Insert the blade of a knife and if it comes out clean, the cake is cooked.

Elizabeth

'This absolutely delicious cake came from a very modest reader who just gave me her first name and no address.'

Preparation Time:	20 minutes
Cooking Time:	45 minutes
Oven Temperature:	180°C/350°F/Gas Mark 4
Reader's Tip:	If you want to make a larger, 1 kg/2 lb cake, double the quantities and use the appropriate loaf tin, and bake for 1–1¼ hours

4
SMALL CAKES AND BISCUITS

Rock Cakes

125 g/4 oz margarine
250 g/8 oz self-raising flour,
   sifted
a pinch of salt

50 g/2 oz caster sugar
1 egg
a little milk

❶ Grease a baking sheet and preheat the oven to 200°C/400°F/Gas Mark 6.

❷ Rub the margarine into the flour and salt. Stir in the sugar. Mix in the egg and milk to make a soft dough.

❸ Fork dollops of the mixture, about the size of a small egg, on to the prepared baking sheet. Sprinkle with a little caster sugar.

❹ Bake in the preheated oven for 15–20 minutes until pale brown.

E. Ridout,
New Malden, Essex

Makes 12–14 cakes, depending on size
Preparation Time: 10 minutes
Cooking Time: 15–20 minutes
Oven Temperature: 200°C/400°F/Gas Mark 6

Reader's Tip: An optional extra is to include about 125 g/4 oz dried mixed fruit in the cake mixture.

IDIOT BISCUITS

75 g/3 oz butter, softened   1 tablespoon cocoa powder,
50 g/2 oz caster sugar   sifted
$^1/_2$ teaspoon vanilla essence
125 g/4 oz plain flour, sifted

❶ Lightly grease a baking sheet and preheat the oven to 160°C/325°F/Gas Mark 3.

❷ Cream together the butter and sugar until pale and fluffy. Add the vanilla essence, and stir in the flour and cocoa powder.

❸ Use your hands to bring the dough together. When the mixture is in one solid lump, roll into small balls. Arrange these on a baking sheet and press down lightly with a fork dipped in water (hot or cold).

❹ Bake in the preheated oven for 20–30 minutes.

Jo Haines,
Great Dunmow, Essex

Makes 16 biscuits

Preparation Time: 15 minutes
Cooking Time: 20–30 minutes
Oven Temperature: 160°C/325°F/Gas Mark 3

Reader's Tip: Simply soften the butter by leaving it
                       for a while at room temperature in a
                       warm room. The obvious choice is
                       the kitchen.

Fruit Scones

250 g/8 oz self-raising flour
1/2 teaspoon salt
40 g/11/2 oz butter or
  margarine
50 g/2 oz sugar
50 g/2 oz sultanas or
  currants
about 150 ml/1/4 pint milk

❶ Grease a baking sheet and preheat the oven to 200°C/400°F/Gas Mark 6.

❷ Sift together the flour and salt into a bowl, then add the butter or margarine, and crumble together until the mixture resembles fine breadcrumbs. Add the sugar and fruit and just enough milk to make a fairly stiff dough. Roll the dough into a ball.

❸ Roll out on a floured surface until about 1 cm/1/2 inch thick, then cut into rounds with a 5 cm/2 inch cutter.

❹ Arrange these on the prepared baking sheet and bake in the preheated oven for about 10–12 minutes.

❺ When the scones are cool, cut them in half horizontally and butter.

Muriel Allan
Sunderland

'*There is something very comforting in cold weather about scones straight out of the oven for tea. The recipe for these scones has been in the family for generations, and my Grandpa grew up on them. We all love them too.*'

	Makes 16 x 5 cm/2 inch scones
Preparation Time:	10 minutes
Cooking Time:	10–12 minutes
Oven Temperature:	200°C/400°F/Gas Mark 6
Reader's Tip:	To make cheese scones, omit the sugar and fruit, and add 50–75 g/2–3 oz grated cooking cheese. For a glazed top, brush the scones with beaten egg before baking them. It is worth noting that scones freeze particularly well.

GRANNY'S EASTER BISCUITS

125 g/4 oz butter or
  margarine
75 g/3 oz caster sugar
2 egg yolks
250 g/8 oz self-raising flour
a pinch of mixed spice
a pinch of cinnamon
50 g/2 oz sultanas
1 egg white, beaten, for
  brushing
caster sugar, for sprinkling

❶ Butter one or two baking sheets and preheat the oven
to 180°C/350°F/Gas Mark 4.

❷ Cream together the butter or margarine and sugar. Add
the egg yolks, 1 at a time, and beat thoroughly. Add the
flour, mixed spice, cinnamon and sultanas. Knead well.

❸ Roll out on a floured board to about 5 mm/$\frac{1}{4}$ inch
thick. Cut into rounds with a 5 cm/2 inch cutter. Re-
roll any leftover dough and cut again.

4 Place on the greased baking sheets, brush with egg white, and sprinkle with caster sugar.

5 Bake in the centre of the preheated oven for 10–15 minutes, until golden brown.

Mary Dyson
Truro, Cornwall

	Makes 20–25 biscuits
Preparation Time:	15 minutes
Cooking Time:	10–15 minutes
Oven Temperature:	180°C/350°F/Gas Mark 4
Reader's Tip:	This biscuit recipe is perfect for children – both to make and to eat.

RICH FUDGE BROWNIES

125 g/4 oz plain chocolate
50 g/2 oz butter, chopped
2 medium eggs, beaten
175 g/6 oz caster sugar
1 teaspoon vanilla essence
75 g/3 oz self-raising flour,
  sifted
50 g/2 oz walnuts or pecan
  nuts, roughly chopped

1 Butter and line a 20 cm/8 inch square cake tin. Preheat the oven to 180°C/350°F/Gas Mark 4.

2 Melt the chocolate in a heatproof bowl over boiling water. Add the butter and stir until the butter is melted. Remove from the heat and allow to cool.

3 Beat the eggs, caster sugar and vanilla essence well together, add to the chocolate and beat again.

4 Fold in the flour, using a large metal spoon. Then stir in the chopped nuts.

5 Pour the mixture into the prepared cake tin and bake for 25–40 minutes.

❻ Allow to cool in the tin for 10 minutes. Then cut into squares and turn out on to a cooling rack.

Karin Smith
Reading, Berkshire

'These chocolate brownies are deliciously
wicked and should be administered
on grey days when only chocolate can help.'

Preparation Time: 15 minutes
Cooking Time: 25–40 minutes
Oven Temperature: 180°C/350°F/Gas Mark 4

Reader's Tip: Exactly how long you cook these brownies for depends on how you like them. If you like them very fudgy and gooey in the centre, cook them for just 25 minutes. If you like them firm and dry, cook them for longer. You can also add plain, milk or white chocolate chunks.

CHOCOLATE GOODIES

125 g/4 oz digestive biscuits   3 tablespoons chocolate
125 g/4 oz margarine   powder
1 tablespoon caster sugar   a handful of sultanas
1 tablespoon golden syrup   plain cooking chocolate

1. Grease a large baking sheet.

2. Put the digestive biscuits in a polythene bag and crush them roughly with a rolling pin until they form large crumbs.

3. Melt the margarine, add all the remaining ingredients except for the chocolate, and mix well.

4. Press the biscuit mixture firmly on to the greased baking sheet. Allow to set in the refrigerator for at least 1 hour.

5. Meanwhile, melt the chocolate and pour over the set biscuit mixture. Return to the refrigerator to set and cut into pieces when cooled.

Mary Dyson
Truro, Cornwall

Preparation Time:	15 minutes
Reader's Tip:	If you like dates, use chopped dates instead of sultanas. Another possibility is to use a mixture of sultanas and dates.

GRANNY'S BISCUITS

125 g/4 oz hard margarine
1 dessertspoon golden syrup
125 g/4 oz self-raising flour
50 g/2 oz porridge oats

1/2 teaspoon bicarbonate of
 soda
75 g/3 oz demerara sugar
1/2 teaspoon mixed spice

❶ Grease a baking sheet and preheat the oven to 180°C/350°F/Gas Mark 4.

❷ Melt the margarine and syrup in a saucepan. Pour this on to all the other ingredients in a mixing bowl, and mix well.

❸ Roll the biscuit dough into small balls and flatten these on a baking sheet, allowing enough room for them to expand.

❹ Bake in the preheated oven for 10–15 minutes and leave to cool slightly before removing them from the tray.

Pam Whitwam
Reading, Berkshire

	Makes 16–18 biscuits
Preparation Time:	5 minutes
Cooking Time:	10–15 minutes
Oven Temperature:	180°C/350°F/Gas Mark 4
Reader's Tip:	This is a very easy recipe and therefore a good one for children to make, as long as help is given with pouring the hot margarine and syrup into the mixing bowl.

EASY ECCLES CAKES

375 g/12 oz puff pastry, thawed if frozen

25 g/1 oz granulated sugar

Filling
1 tablespoon melted butter
125 g/4 oz soft brown sugar

125 g/4 oz currants or seedless raisins
$1/_2$ teaspoon cinnamon
$1/_4$ teaspoon ground nutmeg
50 g/2 oz candied peel
grated rind of 1 lemon

❶ Grease a baking tray and preheat the oven to 230°C/450°F/Gas Mark 8.

❷ Roll out the pastry thinly and cut into 12 cm/5 inch squares.

❸ Mix together all the filling ingredients and place a heaped teaspoon of this mixture in the centre of each pastry square. Lightly damp the pastry edges, bring the edges up to the centre and pinch together.

❹ Turn the parcels over and mould them into round shapes. Roll with a rolling pin until the cakes are about 6 cm/$2^1/_2$ inches in diameter and the fruit shows through the pastry.

5 Repeat until all the ingredients have been used up. Dampen the tops and sprinkle with the sugar.

6 Place all the cakes on the prepared baking try and cut three slits in the top of each one. Bake in the preheated oven for 10–15 minutes until lightly browned.

Pam Whitwam
Reading, Berkshire

'I think these are
nostalgia cakes.
They are what we had
at Granny's when
we were little.'

Preparation Time:	20 minutes
Cooking Time:	10–15 minutes
Oven Temperature:	230°C/450°F/Gas Mark 8
Reader's Tip:	Eccles cakes may also be made using flaky or rough puff pastry, as you prefer. Either way, they're delicious.

MOCK FLORENTINE BARS

175 g/6 oz plain chocolate
125 g/4 oz soft margarine
175 g/6 oz caster sugar
2 eggs
125 g/4 oz glacé cherries,
  chopped
125 g/4 oz sultanas
150 g/5 oz porridge oats
75 g/3 oz desiccated coconut

❶ Grease and line a 23 x 33 cm/9 x 13 inch Swiss roll tin with greaseproof paper, or use a 20 cm/8 inch square tin. Preheat the oven to 180°C/350°F/Gas Mark 4.

❷ Melt the chocolate in a basin over a pan of hot water, then spread this evenly over the paper in the tin. Chill until the chocolate has set.

❸ Cream together the margarine and sugar until light and fluffy. Gradually add the eggs, beating well after each addition.

❹ Mix in the cherries, sultanas, oats and desiccated coconut. Spread this mixture over the chocolate.

❺ Bake in the centre of the preheated oven for 25–35 minutes until golden brown. Leave in the tin until completely cold, then invert on to a board, peel off the paper and cut into 24 bars.

Judy Cairns
Hemdon, Northamptonshire

> *'These are good served with coffee after dinner and more original than a box of After Eights.'*

	Makes 24 bars
Preparation Time:	15 minutes
Cooking Time:	25–35 minutes
Oven Temperature:	180°C/350°F/Gas Mark 4
Reader's Tip:	Use a plain chocolate that has at least 70% cocoa solids. You will find the percentage of cocoa solids stated on the wrapper. If these biscuits fall apart when you cut them, put the whole block in the freezer until they are hard enough to cut more easily.

CRUNCHY LEMON SQUARES

150 g/5 oz caster sugar
150 g/5 oz self-raising flour, sifted
150 g/5 oz soft margarine
1 heaped teaspoon baking powder

grated rind and juice of 1 lemon
2–3 eggs, beaten, measured to 125 ml/4 fl oz
3 tablespoons granulated sugar

❶ Grease and line an 18 x 23 x 2.5 cm/7 x 9 x 1 inch baking tray and preheat the oven to 180°C/350°F/Gas Mark 4.

❷ Put the caster sugar, flour, margarine, baking powder, lemon rind and eggs in a large mixing bowl and stir well to combine thoroughly.

❸ Turn the mixture into the baking tray and smooth the surface. Bake in the centre of the preheated oven for about 30 minutes, until the cake is well risen and pale gold in colour and springs back when pressed in the centre.

❹ Meanwhile, mix the lemon juice with the granulated sugar and spoon this over the cake while it is still hot. Leave in the baking tray until completely cold, then turn out and cut into 12 squares.

Angela Master
Royston, Hertfordshire

Preparation Time:	25 minutes
Cooking Time:	30 minutes
Oven Temperature:	180°C/350°F/Gas Mark 4
Reader's Tip:	This cake freezes well, if you'd like to save it for later.

5
CHOCOLATE CAKES

CHOCOLATE CAKE WITH ORANGE SYRUP

200 g/7 oz self-raising flour
2 tablespoons drinking
   chocolate powder
250 g/8 oz caster sugar
$^3/_4$ teaspoon salt
125 g/4 oz soft margarine or
   butter
1 teaspoon vanilla essence
2 eggs, beaten with 175 ml/
6 fl oz milk

Syrup
rind and juice of 1 orange
125 g/4 oz sugar

❶ Grease and line an oblong 1 kg/2 lb loaf tin. Preheat the oven to 180°C/350°F/Gas Mark 4.

❷ Sift together the flour, drinking chocolate, sugar and salt.

❸ Rub in the margarine or butter.

❹ Add the vanilla essence and milk, and beat well.

❺ Pour the cake mixture into the prepared loaf tin and bake in the preheated oven for about 1 hour.

❻ To make the orange syrup, put the orange rind and juice and the sugar in a pan, bring to the boil and continue to boil until the mixture is thick.

7 While the cake is still hot, make slits across the top of the cake and pour over the orange syrup. Allow to cool completely before turning out on to a plate.

Lindsey Appleby
Reading, Berkshire

'The flavours of chocolate and orange are perfect partners.'

Preparation Time:	20 minutes
Cooking Time:	1 hour
Oven Temperature:	180°C/350°F/Gas Mark 4
Reader's Tip:	This is quite a wet cake mixture, so be sure not to use a loose-bottomed cake tin.

One–Bowl Chocolate Cake

125 g/4 oz butter, softened
125 g/4 oz caster sugar
125 g/4 oz self-raising flour,
  sifted
2 tablespoons drinking
  chocolate

1 teaspoon cocoa
1 teaspoon baking powder
2 eggs
2 tablespoons cold milk
1/2 teaspoon vanilla essence

❶ Grease and line two 15 cm/6 inch cake tins and preheat the oven to 190°C/375°F/Gas Mark 5.

❷ Put all the ingredients in a food processor and whizz until smooth.

❸ Turn the cake mixture into the prepared cake tins and bake in the preheated oven for 20–30 minutes or until well risen, firm to the touch and beginning to shrink away from the sides.

❹ Turn the cake out on to a cooling rack and allow it to cool.

Heather Baker
Bognor Regis, West Sussex

Preparation Time:	20 minutes
Cooking Time:	20–30 minutes
Oven Temperature:	190°C/375°F/Gas Mark 5
Reader's Tip:	To use this mixture for fairy cakes, increase the oven temperature to 200°C/400°F/Gas Mark 6 and reduce the cooking time to 15–20 minutes.

CHOCOLATE BISCUIT CAKE

1 tablespoon golden syrup
150 g/5 oz butter
1 tablespoon sugar
2 tablespoons cocoa powder
275 g/9 oz digestive biscuits,
  crushed

25 g/1 oz ground almonds
2 teaspoons coffee essence
25 g/1 oz sultanas (optional)

❶ Grease a shallow oven tray.

❷ Place the golden syrup in a saucepan with the butter and sugar, and warm gently over low heat. Remove from the heat and then add the cocoa, biscuit crumbs, ground almonds, coffee essence and sultanas, if using.

❸ Press the mixture into the prepared oven tray, using the back of a spoon. Refrigerate for a few hours and then slice.

Anne Larpent
Ross-on-Wye, Herefordshire

Preparation Time: 10 minutes

Reader's Tip: If you have a food processor, crush the biscuits and then add all the other ingredients and whizz until the mixture comes together. This cake freezes well, in which case it should be thawed at room temperature for 2–3 hours before eating. A finishing touch is to melt 75 g/3 oz plain chocolate and pour it evenly over the cake to set – millions of calories but absolutely wonderful.

ONE–STAGE CHOCOLATE CAKE

125 g/4 oz soft margarine
150 g/5 oz caster sugar
150 g/5 oz self-raising flour
1 tablespoon cocoa powder
2 large eggs
2 tablespoons milk
$1/2$ teaspoon vanilla essence

Filling
50 g/2 oz soft margarine
50 g/2 oz icing sugar
50 g/2 oz drinking chocolate

❶ Grease and line two round sandwich cake tins and pre-heat the oven to 200°C/400°F/Gas Mark 6.

❷ Put all the ingredients in a bowl and blend together with an electric mixer. Pour into the cake tins, smooth over the tops and bake in the preheated oven for 15 minutes, until risen and firm to the touch. Run a knife around the tins and tip upside down on to a cooling rack.

❸ Meanwhile, mix together all the filling ingredients with a wooden spoon until soft and creamy. When the cake is cool, sandwich the cakes with half the filling and spread the rest on top of the cake.

Anne Dean
Altrincham, Cheshire

Preparation Time:	20 minutes
Cooking Time:	15 minutes
Oven Temperature:	200°C/400°F/Gas Mark 6
Reader's Tip:	An alternative filling, if you prefer, is to use jam – in any flavour that you really like.

Foolproof Chocolate Cake

250 g/8 oz self-raising flour
25 g/1 oz cocoa powder
1/2 teaspoon salt
125 g/4 oz butter or hard
  margarine, softened
200 g/7 oz caster sugar
3 eggs

5 tablespoons water
5 tablespoons condensed
  milk
1/2 teaspoon vanilla essence

❶ Grease and line two shallow 18 cm/7 inch cake tins.
Preheat the oven to 180°C/350°F/Gas Mark 4.

❷ Sift together the flour, cocoa powder and salt. Rub in
the butter or margarine until the mixture looks like fine
breadcrumbs, with no big lumps. Stir in the sugar.

❸ In another bowl, beat together the eggs, water, condensed
milk and vanilla essence. Pour this mixture into the flour
mixture and mix until there are no dry bits visible.

❹ Pour the cake mixture into the prepared cake tins and
bake in the preheated oven for about 25–30 minutes.
Remove from the oven and leave for 10 minutes before
turning out on to a cake rack to cool completely.

5 Sandwich the cakes together with jam, butter cream or whipped fresh cream, as you prefer. A nice finishing touch is to pour melted chocolate over the cake, if liked.

Helen Kaczmarczuk
Dunstable, Bedfordshire

'This recipe cannot fail. A perfect quick birthday cake.'

Preparation Time:	15 minutes
Cooking Time:	25–30 minutes
Oven Temperature:	180°C/350°F/Gas Mark 4
Reader's Tip:	Be sure that you use cocoa powder – not drinking chocolate – to make this recipe. It's so much better.

AMERICAN CHOCOLATE CAKE

300 g/10 oz self-raising flour
$1/2$ teaspoon salt
3 tablespoons cocoa
175 g/6 oz caster sugar
1 teaspoon bicarbonate of soda
300 ml/$1/2$ pint milk
150 ml/$1/4$ pint corn oil

1 tablespoon golden syrup
3 teaspoons vanilla essence

Chocolate icing
40 g/$1^1/2$ oz butter
25 g/1 oz cocoa, sifted
3 tablespoons milk
125 g/4 oz icing sugar

❶ Grease and line two 20 cm/8 inch sandwich tins with greased greaseproof paper. Preheat the oven to 180°C/350°F/Gas Mark 4.

❷ Sift the flour, salt, cocoa and sugar into a mixing bowl and make a well in the centre.

❸ Dissolve the bicarbonate of soda in 1 tablespoon of the milk and pour this into the well, with the remaining milk, oil, golden syrup and vanilla essence, and beat well to make a smooth batter.

❹ Pour the cake mixture into the prepared cake tins and bake in the preheated oven for about 35–40 minutes, or until the cakes spring back when lightly pressed with a fingertip.

❺ Meanwhile, make the chocolate icing. Melt the butter in a small saucepan and stir in the cocoa, and cook over a low heat for 1 minute. Remove from the heat and add the milk and icing sugar. Beat well to mix and then leave to cool, stirring occasionally until the icing has thickened to a spreading consistency.

❻ When the cakes are cooked, turn them out on to a wire cooling rack and leave to cool.

❼ Sandwich the two cakes together with chocolate icing, and put more icing on top of the cake.

Anon

*'Administer this cake to chocoholics –
liberally and frequently.'*

Preparation Time:	10 minutes
Cooking Time:	35–40 minutes
Oven Temperature:	180°C/350°F/Gas Mark 4
Reader's Tip:	Sunflower oil will work just as well as corn oil if that's what you have in your kitchen cupboard.

Chocolate Truffle Cake

475 g/15 oz plain chocolate
100 g/3½ oz butter
150 g/5 oz caster sugar
2 teaspoons coffee granules
4 eggs, separated

40 g/1½ oz plain flour
25 g/1 oz toasted ground
    hazelnuts

1 Grease and line a 22 cm/8½ inch cake tin. Preheat the oven to 160°C/325°F/Gas Mark 3.

2 Melt the chocolate in a bain–marie. Cream together the butter and sugar.

3 Dissolve the coffee in warm water. Beat together the coffee, the butter mixture, the chocolate and the 4 egg yolks.

4 Whisk the egg whites and fold into the mixture. Fold in the flour and nuts.

5 Bake in the preheated oven for 1¼ hours.

Ann Meddings
Kingston, Surrey

Preparation Time:	20 minutes
Cooking Time:	1¼ hours
Oven Temperature:	160°C/325°F/Gas Mark 3
Reader's Tip:	As always, use the best-quality plain chocolate, with at least 70% cocoa solids. Less than that will not achieve such good results.

Pfister Cake

150 g/5 oz butter
265 g/8½ oz caster sugar
5 eggs, separated
150 g/5 oz ground almonds
150 g/5 oz dark chocolate,

broken into very small
pieces
100 g/3½ oz self-raising
flour, sifted

❶ Grease and line a 20 cm/8 inch cake tin and preheat the oven to 180°C/350°F/Gas Mark 4.

❷ Beat together the butter and sugar until white.

❸ Add the egg yolks and almonds, then add the chocolate pieces and mix well. Fold in the flour.

❹ Beat the egg whites until stiff, then fold into the mixture using a metal spoon. Mix well but do not beat.

❺ Put the mixture in the prepared cake tin and bake in the preheated oven for 50 minutes–1 hour.

❻ Turn out on to a cooling rack and allow to cool completely.

Betty Jones
Cyncoed, Cardiff

Preparation Time:	20 minutes
Cooking Time:	50 minutes–1 hour
Oven Temperature:	180°C/350°F/Gas Mark 4
Reader's Tip:	Store this cake in aluminium foil for at least a week before serving. It gets better and better!

CHOCOLATE MOSAIC

250 g/8 oz rich tea biscuits
3 tablespoons chocolate
  spread
2 tablespoons golden syrup
50 g/2 oz butter
1/2 teaspoon ground ginger
2 eggs
150 ml/1/4 pint double cream
grated chocolate, to
  decorate

❶ Grease and line a 500 g/1 lb loaf tin with clingfilm, making sure it comes up and over the sides.

❷ Place the biscuits in a plastic bag and crush into small pieces with a rolling pin.

❸ Put the chocolate spread, golden syrup, butter and ground ginger in a saucepan, and blend them together over a gentle heat.

❹ Whisk the eggs and add to the chocolate mixture, stirring well as the eggs cook to keep the mixture really smooth.

❺ Remove from the heat and stir in the biscuit pieces, making sure that they are evenly coated.

6. Press the mixture into the prepared loaf tin and place in the refrigerator for several hours, preferably overnight.

7. Meanwhile, whip the double cream until stiff.

8. Turn out the chocolate cake, cover with whipped cream and decorate with grated chocolate.

Pat Brown
Reading, Berkshire

'This is simple and quick to make, yet rich and impressive.'

CHOCOLATE ORANGE CHIP CAKE

125 g/4 oz butter or
   margarine
125 g/4 oz caster sugar
1 tablespoon grated orange
   rind
2 eggs

150 g/5 oz self-raising flour,
   sifted
1 tablespoon chopped
   chocolate or chocolate chips
50 g/2 oz walnuts
1 tablespoon orange juice

❶ Grease and line an 18 cm/7 inch cake tin and preheat
   the oven to 180°C/350°F/Gas Mark 4.

❷ Place the butter or margarine, sugar and orange rind in
   a mixing bowl. Beat for 3 minutes until light and fluffy.

❸ Add the eggs, 1 at a time, and beat for 1 minute more.

❹ Add the flour, chocolate, nuts and orange juice, and mix well.

❺ Turn the mixture into the prepared cake tin and bake in
   the preheated oven for 25–30 minutes until the cake
   springs back when touched lightly.

Miss J.C. Turner
Hook, Hampshire

Preparation Time:	15 minutes
Cooking Time:	25–30 minutes
Oven Temperature:	180°C/350°F/Gas Mark 4
Reader's Tip:	Chocolate and orange are a great combination of flavours made in heaven.

CHOCOLATE CAKE

125 g/4 oz hard margarine
125 g/4 oz soft brown sugar
2 tablespoons golden syrup
175 g/6 oz self-raising flour
60 g/2¹/₂ oz cocoa

1 egg
150 ml/¹/₄ pint milk
¹/₂ teaspoon bicarbonate of
  soda

1 Grease and line two 20 cm/8 inch sandwich tins.
Preheat the oven to 190°C/375°F/Gas Mark 5.

2 Melt the margarine, sugar and syrup in a saucepan over
a gentle heat. Transfer to a large mixing bowl and pour
over the flour and cocoa. Mix together well. Add the
egg and stir again.

3 Warm the milk slightly, stir in the bicarbonate of soda
and pour this on to the other ingredients, which will
now be very runny.

4 Pour the cake mixture into the prepared cake tins and
bake in the preheated oven for about 30 minutes. Turn
out on to a cooling rack and allow to cool.

Pam Whitwam
Reading, Berkshire

Preparation Time: 15 minutes
Cooking Time: 30 minutes
Oven Temperature: 190°C/375°F/Gas Mark 5

Reader's Tip: Sandwich the cakes together with
                           chocolate or coffee butter icing. On
                           special occasions, top with
                           chocolate icing and walnuts.

CHOCOLATE WALNUT CAKE

250 g/8 oz plain chocolate
250 g/8 oz butter or
  margarine
2 eggs
2 tablespoons caster sugar
250 g/8 oz digestive biscuits
40 g/1¹/₂ oz chopped
  walnuts, plus a little extra
  to decorate

40 g/1¹/₂ oz glacé cherries,
  plus a few extra, halved, to
  decorate
1 tablespoon brandy or rum

❶ Butter an 18 cm/7 inch cake tin with a removable base.

❷ Melt the chocolate in a bowl over a pan of boiling water. While the chocolate is softening, melt the butter or margarine in another pan.

❸ Beat the eggs and add the caster sugar. Pour the melted butter into the egg mixture in a steady stream, stirring continuously. Add the melted chocolate and beat this in.

❹ Break the digestive biscuits into small pieces, and stir these into the mixture. Then add the walnuts, the glacé cherries, and the brandy or rum.

⑤ Transfer the mixture to the prepared cake tin, and decorate with the reserved walnuts and glacé cherries. Refrigerate until needed.

Gloria Cann
White Waltham, Berkshire

Preparation Time:	15 minutes
Reader's Tip:	One of the joys of this cake is that it does not require any cooking. Simply refrigerate it until ready to serve.

QUICK CHOCOLATE CAKE

125 g/4 oz self-raising flour
25 g/1 oz cocoa or carob
  powder
150 g/5 oz caster sugar
150 g/5 oz soft margarine
3 eggs
1 teaspoon baking powder
1 tablespoon hot water

Chocolate Filling and
  Topping
200 g/7 oz cooking chocolate
  or carob bar
2 tablespoons milk

❶ Grease and line two 18 cm/7 inch sandwich tins. Preheat the oven to 180°C/350°F/Gas Mark 4.

❷ Sieve the flour and cocoa or carob powder into a mixing bowl. Add all the other ingredients and beat well until smooth and shiny.

❸ Divide the cake mixture between the two prepared sandwich tins and bake in the preheated oven for 25–30 minutes until the cakes spring back when they are touched lightly.

❹ Meanwhile, make the chocolate filling and topping. Cut the chocolate into small pieces and place it, or the carob powder, in a bowl over a pan of hot water to melt. Remove from the heat and add the milk, 1 tablespoon at a time, until the mixture thickens.

5 When the cake is cooked, turn out on to a cooling rack and allow to cool. Sandwich and top the cake with the prepared chocolate filling and topping.

Miss J.C. Turner
Hook, Hampshire

'This recipe is easy to make,
quick to cook, and tends
to disappear rapidly from the plate.'

Preparation Time:	20 minutes
Cooking Time:	25–30 minutes
Oven Temperature:	180°C/350°F/Gas Mark 4
Reader's Tip:	Chocolate does not agree with everybody and some people are actually allergic to it. Carob, which comes from the carob tree that grows all over the Mediterranean and in the US, is considered by some people to be a healthier alternative – high in vitamins and minerals and free from caffeine.

Summer Cake

125 g/4 oz margarine	1¹/₂ tablespoons cocoa
1 tablespoon golden syrup	75 g/3 oz cornflakes
1 tablespoon sugar	

❶ Grease a shallow 18 cm/7 inch cake tin, and line the greased tin with clingfilm so that it will be easy to remove the cake.

❷ Slowly melt the margarine with the syrup and sugar in a large saucepan.

❸ Stir in the cocoa, then add the cornflakes and stir well.

❹ Transfer the cake mixture to the prepared cake tin and leave to set in the refrigerator.

Lindy Moffatt
Hadlow Down, Sussex

Preparation Time:	15 minutes
Reader's Tip:	This is an excellent recipe to start children off in the kitchen. You can experiment with their different favourite breakfast cereals and discover which works best. You can also, if you prefer, use individual cup cases instead of a large cake tin.

BISCUIT CAKE

250 g/8 oz rich tea biscuits	1 tablespoon caster sugar
125 g/4 oz margarine	50 g/2 oz sultanas
2 teaspoons cocoa	125 g/4 oz plain chocolate
1–2 tablespoons golden syrup	

1 Grease and line an 18 cm/7 inch or 20 cm/8 inch cake tin with clingfilm, so that it comes up over the sides of the tin.

2 Crush the biscuits by putting them in a polythene bag and pressing with a rolling pin. They can be crushed as coarsely or as finely as you like.

3 Put the margarine, cocoa, golden syrup, sugar and sultanas in a large saucepan. Heat over a gentle heat and bring to the boil, then mix in the biscuits.

4 Press the mixture into the prepared cake tin. Melt the chocolate in a bowl over hot water and then pour over the cake. Leave to set in the refrigerator. Just before serving, simply peel away the clingfilm to reveal your perfect cake.

Lindy Moffatt
Hadlow Down, Sussex

Preparation Time:	15 minutes
Reader's Tip:	This biscuit cake is very easy to prepare, and makes an excellent pudding. Serve with cream.

CHOCOLATE LOAF

vegetable oil, for greasing

175 g/6 oz plain cooking
chocolate, broken into
small pieces

50 ml/2 fl oz dark rum

175 g/6 oz unsalted butter,
softened

1 teaspoon sugar

2 eggs, separated

125 g/4 oz ground almonds

75 g/3 oz hazelnuts or
almonds, crushed

$1/_3$ teaspoon salt

300 ml/$1/_2$ pint double cream,
whipped, to cover

❶ Line a 1.5 kg/3 lb loaf tin or a 20 cm/8 inch round cake tin with greaseproof paper, leaving some of the paper overlapping the tin. Then grease the paper with the vegetable oil and stand the tin upside down on kitchen paper to drain.

❷ Melt the chocolate in a basin over hot water, stirring continuously. Then stir in the rum. Remove from the heat and set aside to cool.

❸ In a large bowl, cream together the butter and sugar, using a wooden spoon, until smooth and pale. Beat in the egg yolks and ground almonds. Then add the chocolate mixture and beat again. Mix in the crushed nuts.

❹ Whisk the egg whites with the salt until they form stiff peaks.

⑤ Using a metal spoon, carefully fold the egg whites into the chocolate mixture.

⑥ Spoon the cake mixture into the prepared loaf tin and spread out evenly with a palette knife.

⑦ Cover the tin with aluminium foil and put in the refrigerator to chill for at least 5 hours or until the loaf is firm, preferably overnight.

⑧ To unmould the loaf, loosen the sides with a knife and quickly dip the tin into hot water. Turn out the cake over a serving plate.

⑨ Cover with cream and slice the loaf thinly.

Delia Gaze
Deptford, London

'This is a good alternative to Christmas Cake for those who do not like fruit cake.'

Preparation Time:	40 minutes, plus at least 5 hours chilling time
Reader's Tip:	If you have a microwave, this is the perfect way to melt the chocolate.

KAROLYI TORTA

8 eggs, separated
200 g/7 oz icing sugar
150 g/5 oz best quality plain
  chocolate, broken into pieces
140 g/4½ oz slightly salted
  butter
2–4 tablespoons lukewarm
  water
1 tablespoon Tia Maria
15 g/½ oz vanilla sugar
150 g/5 oz ground hazelnuts
  or almonds

Filling and Topping
425 g/14 oz apricot preserve
1–2 tablespoons Cointreau
300 ml/½ pint whipping cream
15 g/½ oz vanilla sugar
1 tablespoon icing sugar
125 g/4 oz chocolate
25 g/1 oz butter
1–2 tablespoons Tia Maria
a pinch of instant coffee

❶ Line two large round baking tins with greaseproof paper. Preheat the oven to 150°C/300°F/Gas Mark 2.

❷ Beat the egg whites until they are just beginning to stiffen, then add about one-third of the icing sugar, bit by bit, until the egg whites just hold their shape.

❸ Melt the broken chocolate pieces with the butter, 1–2 tablespoons lukewarm water and the Tia Maria in a bowl over hot water.

❹ Beat the egg yolks with the remaining sugar, the vanilla sugar and 1–2 tablespoons lukewarm water until thick and frothy. Slowly add the cooled chocolate and butter mixture, and add the ground nuts. Then carefully fold in the egg whites.

5 Pour the cake mixture into the prepared cake tins and bake for about 40–50 minutes, or until a metal skewer inserted into the centre comes out clean. Allow the cake to cool in the tin, then turn out on to a cooling rack.

6 Mix the apricot preserve with the Cointreau, and spread the cakes with this mixture.

7 Beat the cream, gradually adding the two sugars as it stiffens.

8 Melt the chocolate and butter in a bowl over hot water. Add the Tia Maria and instant coffee.

9 Sandwich the cakes together with some of the cream, then pile the rest on the top and sides of the cake. Swirl the melted chocolate through the cream with the prongs of a fork to make a pretty pattern.

Elisabeth Wengersky
South Hampstead, London

'Choose a really superior apricot jam, with at least 40% fruit.'

Preparation Time:	30 minutes
Cooking Time:	40–50 minutes
Oven Temperature:	150°C/300°F/Gas Mark 2
Reader's Tip:	For the best flavour, keep this delicious Hungarian cake in the refrigerator for 1 day before eating. It can also be frozen for up to 2 weeks.

6
PARTY CAKES

Auntie Glad's Bakewell Tart

125 g/4 oz shortcut pastry
  (thawed if frozen)
raspberry jam, to taste, for
  spreading
275 g/9 oz ground rice
275 g/9 oz caster sugar

275 g/9 oz butter, softened,
  or soft margarine
3 eggs
$\frac{1}{2}$ teaspoon almond essence
a little cold water or milk
  (optional)

❶ Grease three deep 18 cm/7 inch pie plates – one to eat
and two to freeze, though they are unlikely to stay in the
freezer for very long before prying fingers have raided
it. Preheat the oven to 200°C/400°F/Gas Mark 6.

❷ Roll the shortcust pastry thinly and line the pie plates
with it. Spread the pastry as thinly or as thickly as you
like with raspberry jam.

❸ Beat together the ground rice, caster sugar, butter or
margarine, eggs and almond essence to a smooth paste.
If the mixture is too stiff, add a little cold water or milk,
as you prefer.

❹ Divide the mixture between the three tins and smooth
the surface with a palette knife.

⑤ Bake in the preheated oven for about 30 minutes or until the pastry is golden brown and the filling is firm to the touch.

⑥ Serve hot or cold with custard or cream.

Rev. Raymond Smith
Shrewsbury, Shropshire

'Here is a recipe that really does work and is absolutely gorgeous. There was a lovely old lady in one of my first churches who was as far round as she was high and had a highly polished black leaded grate on which she cooked the most divine cakes and pastries. I got this recipe from her and after our first son was born she became "Auntie Glad" - hence the name of the recipe.'

Preparation Time:	20 minutes
Cooking Time:	30 minutes
Oven Temperature:	200°C/400°F/Gas Mark 6
Reader's Tip:	This recipe uses ground rice rather than ground almonds – this is a lot cheaper and tastes just as good provided, of course, that you don't forget to add the almond essence.

WHISKY CAKE

175 g/6 oz sultanas
125 g/4 oz butter
125 g/4 oz caster sugar
1 egg
1 teaspoon bicarbonate of
  soda

175 g/6 oz plain flour
1/2 teaspoon grated nutmeg
65 g/2 1/2 oz chopped walnuts
1 tablespoon lemon juice
1 tablespoon whisky

❶ Grease and line a 20 cm/8 inch deep-sided cake tin and preheat the oven to 180°C/350°F/Gas Mark 4.

❷ Simmer the sultanas in just enough water to cover for 5–10 minutes. Drain and reserve the cooking liquid.

❸ Beat together the butter and sugar until fluffy. Beat in the egg.

❹ Add the bicarbonate of soda to the flour and sieve into the cake mixture with the nutmeg, cooled sultanas, walnuts, lemon juice and whisky.

❺ Put the mixture into the prepared cake tin and bake in the preheated oven for 45–55 minutes.

Jean Hurley
Ashcombe, Devon

Preparation Time: 20 minutes
Cooking Time: 45–55 minutes
Oven Temperature: 180°C/350°F/Gas Mark 4

Reader's Tip: If the mixture seems a little dry, add
                           some of the sultana cooking liquid.

TREACLE CAKE

300 g/10 oz self-raising flour, sifted
200 g/7 oz caster sugar
165 g/5¹/₂ oz mixed dried fruit

1 egg, beaten
250 ml/8 fl oz milk
2 tablespoons black treacle

❶ Grease and line a 1 kg/2 lb loaf tin with greaseproof paper. Preheat the oven to 180°C/350°F/Gas Mark 4.

❷ Put the flour, sugar and dried fruit in a large mixing bowl. Make a well in the centre and mix in the egg and milk.

❸ Add the black treacle and mix in thoroughly.

❹ Pour the cake mixture into the prepared cake tin. Bake for 1¹/₄ hours until a knife inserted into the centre comes out clean.

Lindy Moffatt
Hadlow Down, Sussex

Preparation Time:	15 minutes
Cooking Time:	1¹/₄ hours
Oven Temperature:	180°C/350°F/Gas Mark 4
Reader's Tip:	You can use golden syrup instead of black treacle. This is rather sweeter but not so rich and will give a slightly lighter flavour.

BLACK FOREST GATEAU

1 heaped tablespoon cocoa
  powder

2 tablespoons hot water

175 g/6 oz caster sugar

175 g/6 oz soft margarine

3 medium eggs

175 g/6 oz self-raising flour,
  sifted

To Assemble

a little Kirsch

morello cherry jam

whipped cream

125 g/4 oz dark chocolate

1 Grease and line two 18 cm/7 inch cake tins. Preheat the oven to 160°C/325°F/Gas Mark 3.

2 Blend the cocoa with the hot water and allow to cool.

3 Cream together the sugar and margarine, preferably using an electric hand mixer, until the mixture becomes white and fluffy. Then add the cocoa mixture.

4 Beat in the first egg and, as you work, stop beating a few times and scrape the mixture from the sides of the bowl. Add a little flour with the second and third eggs to prevent curdling. Then fold in the remaining flour, using a metal tablespoon.

5 Divide the mixture between the two prepared cake tins and smooth over gently using a knife. Bake on the middle shelf of the preheated oven for 20–30 minutes, until the cake is firm, golden brown, and shrinking away slightly from the sides of the tin. Turn out on to a cooling rack and allow to cool completely.

⑥ Cut the two cakes through the middle horizontally and sprinkle on a little Kirsch. Sandwich the two cake halves together with cherry jam. Put the two cakes together with whipped cream between them. Decorate the top with more whipped cream and grate chocolate over the top, using a cheese grater.

Mary Gillies
Ryde, Isle of Wight

'Black Forest Gateau has become the laughing stock of cakes, but most people secretly love it. Tell them it's a 70s retro feast and they'll tuck in.'

Preparation Time:	20–30 minutes
Cooking Time:	20–30 minutes
Oven Temperature:	160°C/325°F/Gas Mark 3
Reader's Tip:	When you are folding in the flour, hold the tablespoon loosely or you will find yourself stirring instead of folding. If the cake seems to be dry or overcooked, moisten it with the juice from a tin of fruit, or sprinkle with a few drops of Kirsch, Amaretto or Cointreau.

STICKY MACAROON CAKE

50 g/2 oz soft margarine
125 g/4 oz caster sugar
125 g/4 oz desiccated
  coconut
1 large egg
3 drops vanilla essence
50 g/2 oz sultanas
50 g/2 oz glacé cherries,
  chopped

25 g/1 oz walnuts, chopped
25 g/1 oz dried pineapple,
  chopped
25 g/1 oz dried papaya,
  chopped
16 squares of plain cooking
  chocolate
chopped walnuts, to
  decorate

❶ Grease and line two 20 cm/8 inch sandwich cake tins with baking parchment. Preheat the oven to 180°C/350°F/Gas Mark 4.

❷ Mix together the margarine, sugar, coconut, egg and vanilla essence. Then add the sultanas, cherries, walnuts, pineapple and papaya.

❸ When all the ingredients are well mixed, divide the mixture between the two prepared cake tins and press down with the back of a fork. Bake in the preheated oven for 20 minutes, or until the top looks golden brown.

❹ Remove the cakes from the oven and gently run the blade of a knife around the edge of the tins. Carefully invert the cakes onto two suitable size plates. The cake will look pale and slightly sticky. Leave it to cool.

5 When the cake is cold, melt the chocolate and cover the pale side of the cake. Scatter with chopped walnuts while the chocolate is still warm.

Doreen Williamson
Hull, East Yorkshire

'This unusual cake is sinfully sticky - guaranteed there won't be anything left on the plate.'

Preparation Time:	30 minutes
Cooking Time:	20 minutes
Oven Temperature:	180°C/350°F/Gas Mark 4
Reader's Tip:	This cake can be made a day or two in advance before you decorate it with chocolate and walnuts.

Walnut Cake

75 g/3 oz walnuts
175 g/6 oz margarine
175 g/6 oz caster sugar
3 eggs
175 g/6 oz self-raising flour,
  sifted

Butter Cream
75 g/3 oz butter
175 g/6 oz icing sugar, sifted
1–2 tablespoons lemon juice

❶ Grease and line two shallow 18 cm/7 inch cake tins. Preheat the oven to 180°C/350°F/Gas Mark 4.

❷ In a food processor or blender, process the walnuts, reserving 9 walnut halves for decorating the cake.

❸ In the food processor or blender, mix the margarine and sugar until creamy, then add the eggs, and then the ground walnuts and flour.

❹ Transfer the cake mixture to the two prepared tins and bake in the preheated oven for 20 minutes. Then turn out the cakes and place on a wire cooling rack.

⑤ Meanwhile, make the butter cream. Cream together the butter and icing sugar, adding the lemon juice to obtain a creamy consistency.

⑥ Sandwich the two cakes with the prepared butter icing and spread some more on the top. Decorate with the reserved walnut halves.

Griselda Hobson
London

'Walnut cake is an acquired taste and yes, I have acquired it.'

Preparation Time:	20 minutes
Cooking Time:	20 minutes
Oven Temperature:	180°C/350°F/Gas Mark 4
Reader's Tip:	Do not be tempted to use margarine to make the butter cream – it will not be nearly as good as if you use butter. Another idea is to omit the walnuts and to add a drop or two of vanilla essence instead. Then sandwich the two cakes with strawberries and whipped cream.

POLISH CAKE

125 g/4 oz margarine
1 tablespoon golden syrup
2 tablespoons drinking
  chocolate
175 g/6 oz plain cooking
  chocolate

Base
250 g/8 oz digestive biscuits
25 g/1 oz margarine or
  butter, melted

❶ Grease a 20 cm/8 inch round cake tin and line with clingfilm so that it comes up and over the sides.

❷ Put the margarine, golden syrup and drinking chocolate in a pan and leave over low heat until all the ingredients are melted.

❸ Now make the base. Crush the digestive biscuits and mix with the melted margarine or butter.

❹ Place the biscuit mixture in the bottom of the cake tin, and pour the prepared syrup mixture on top.

❺ Melt the cooking chocolate in a bowl over hot water. Pour the melted chocolate over the cake and place in the refrigerator until set.

Marion Wilson
Framfield, Sussex

Preparation Time: 15 minutes

Reader's Tip: An easy way to crush digestive biscuits without making a dreadful mess is to place them in a polythene bag and then press a rolling pin over the top until all the biscuits are well broken up.

Moist Lemon Cake

125 g/4 oz soft margarine or
  butter
175 g/6 oz caster sugar
175 g/6 oz self-raising flour
1 teaspoon baking powder
2 large eggs
grated rind of 1 large or 2
  small lemons
65 ml/2½ fl oz milk

Lemon Syrup
3 tablespoons granulated
  sugar
juice of the lemon, or
  lemons, used to make the
  cake

❶ Grease and line a 1 kg/2 lb loaf tin. Preheat the oven to 180°C/350°F/Gas Mark 4.

❷ Place all the cake ingredients in a food processor and blend until really smooth and quite runny.

❸ Pour the cake mixture into the prepared loaf tin and bake in the preheated oven for 45–50 minutes.

❹ Meanwhile, make the lemon syrup. Dissolve the sugar in the lemon juice.

❺ When the cooking time of the cake is up, test that the cake is done by pushing a metal skewer into the centre – if it comes out clean, it's done.

⑥ While the cake is still in the tin, place it on a cooling rack. Prick the cake all over with the skewer and spoon the lemon syrup all over the cake until you have used all the syrup. It will go everywhere, but do not worry – it will set when it is cold. Leave the cake in the tin until it is quite cold.

Pam Daniels
Norwich, Norfolk

'This cake is without question my favourite. It won the Daily Telegraph prize for being the best foolproof cake.'

Preparation Time:	20 minutes
Cooking Time:	45–50 minutes
Oven Temperature:	180°C/350°F/Gas Mark 4
Reader's Tip:	Use free-range eggs for your cakes – they are much better.

COFFEE AND WALNUT CAKE

125 g/4 oz self-raising flour
1 teaspoon baking powder
125 g/4 oz soft brown sugar
125 g/4 oz soft margarine
1 teaspoon coffee essence
2 eggs
25 g/1 oz chopped walnuts

Coffee Frosting
200 g/7 oz icing sugar
40 g/1½ oz butter
2 tablespoons water
25 g/1 oz caster sugar
2 teaspoons coffee essence

❶ Grease and line two 18 cm/7 inch cake tins with grease-proof paper. Preheat the oven to 180°C/350°F/Gas Mark 4.

❷ Sift the flour and baking powder into a mixing bowl. Add the sugar, margarine, coffee essence, eggs and walnuts. Using a wooden spoon, mix to blend the ingredients and then beat well for 1 minute to obtain a smooth cake batter.

❸ Divide the mixture between the prepared cake tins and spread level. Place in the centre of the preheated oven and bake for 25 minutes. Allow to cool in the tin for 2 minutes, then turn out and leave to cool completely.

❹ Meanwhile, make the coffee frosting. Sift the icing sugar into a mixing bowl. Measure the butter, water, sugar and coffee essence into a saucepan and stir over a low heat until the butter has melted and the sugar dissolved.

5 Bring to the boil and pour at once into the sifted ingredients in the mixing bowl. Beat to a smooth glossy icing. Set aside until quite cold, then beat again to make a soft, gooey fudge icing.

6 Sandwich the cake layers with half of the coffee frosting. Spoon the remainder on top. Spread level and then rough up the icing with the tip of a knife to obtain a decorative finish.

Valerie Dunne
Manchester

'Coffee and walnuts marry well. Children might think they're "yucky", though, so don't risk it if you want to win the heart of a five-year-old.'

Preparation Time:	30 minutes
Cooking Time:	25 minutes
Oven Temperature:	180°C/350°F/Gas Mark 4
Reader's Tip:	This scrummy fudge frosting keeps well in the freezer.

ORANGE GINGERBREAD

75 g/3 oz butter
3 tablespoons golden syrup
75 g/3 oz soft brown sugar
175 g/6 oz self-raising flour
1 teaspoon mixed spice
1 teaspoon bicarbonate of
  soda
1½ teaspoons ground ginger
grated rind of 1 orange

1 egg
1 tablespoon orange juice
150 ml/¼ pint water

Orange icing
175 g/6 oz icing sugar
1½ tablespoons orange juice

❶ Grease and line an 18 cm/7 inch cake tin, 5 cm/2 inches deep. Preheat the oven to 160°C/325°F/Gas Mark 3.

❷ Melt the butter, syrup and sugar over a low heat in a saucepan.

❸ Sieve all the dry ingredients and beat in the butter mixture, orange rind and egg.

❹ Boil the orange juice and water in the same pan and beat into the cake mixture.

❺ Transfer the cake mixture into the prepared cake tin and bake in the preheated oven for 1¼–1½ hours. After 45 minutes, cover the top of the cake with two layers of non-stick baking parchment, with a round hole cut in the middle.

6 When the cake is cooked, allow it to cool in the tin.

7 To make the icing, sieve the icing sugar into a mixing bowl and gradually mix in the orange juice. Pour the icing on top of the cake.

J.K.
Pershore, Worcestershire

'The addition of orange rind and juice gives this gingerbread a sharper taste.'

Preparation Time:	30 minutes
Cooking Time:	1¼–1½ hours
Oven Temperature:	160°C/325°F/Gas Mark 3
Reader's Tip:	Use the same quantity of black treacle instead of the golden syrup for a stronger, richer flavour.

FRUIT CRUSTED CIDER CAKE

50 ml/2 fl oz golden syrup
150 g/5 oz butter or hard
  margarine
375 g/12 oz cooking apples,
  peeled, cored and finely
  chopped
50 g/2 oz mincemeat
50 g/2 oz cornflakes, crushed
125 g/4 oz caster sugar

2 eggs, beaten
125 g/4 oz self-raising flour,
  sifted
50 ml/2 fl oz dry cider

❶ Grease and line a 35.5 x 11.5 cm/14 x 4$\frac{1}{2}$ inch shallow rectangular tart frame with aluminium foil. Grease the foil. Preheat the oven to 160°C/325°F/Gas Mark 3.

❷ Put the syrup in a pan with 25 g/1 oz of the butter or margarine, and melt.

❸ Add the apples, mincemeat and cornflakes. Stir together and set aside.

❹ Put the remaining butter and the sugar in a mixing bowl and beat together until pale and fluffy. Gradually beat in the eggs.

❺ Fold the flour into the mixture. Pour in the cider and mix in well.

6 Turn the mixture into the prepared frame and level the surface. Spread the apple mixture evenly over it.

7 Bake in the preheated oven for 45–50 minutes, or until firm to the touch.

8 Cool in the metal frame for 1 hour, then cut into bars for serving.

Gloria Cann
White Waltham

'Apples, cider, mincemeat and cornflakes - the perfect ingredients to make a tasty cake.'

Preparation Time:	30 minutes
Cooking Time:	45–50 minutes
Oven Temperature:	160°C/325°F/Gas Mark 3
Reader's Tip:	Bramleys are the best apples to use for this deliciously succulent cake. The cornflakes add an interesting variation in texture.

RICE CAKE

250 g/8 oz butter, softened   150 g/5 oz ground rice
250 g/8 oz sugar   about 2 tablespoons milk
3 eggs
75 g/3 oz self-raising flour,
  sifted

1 Grease and line a 500 g/1 lb loaf tin with greaseproof paper and preheat the oven to 180°C/350°F/Gas Mark 4.

2 Cream together the butter and sugar until light and creamy. Then stir in the eggs. Fold in the flour and the ground rice. Add just enough milk to produce a soft consistency.

3 When the mixture is well mixed, transfer it to the prepared loaf tin and bake in the preheated oven for 45 minutes–1 hour, until cooked.

4 Turn out on to a cooling rack and allow to cool.

Christine Hill
Cleadon, Tyne and Wear

Preparation Time:	20 minutes
Cooking Time:	45 minutes–1 hour
Oven Temperature:	180°C/350°F/Gas Mark 4
Reader's Tip:	You can add lemon essence instead of milk. This is available in little bottles from grocers and supermarkets. If you don't have any to hand, add a few drops of lemon juice instead.

SHERRY BISCUIT LOG

150 ml/¹/₄ pint double cream　　**1 chocolate flake**
sherry, to taste
1 packet chocolate chip
　biscuits

❶ Whip the cream until stiff.

❷ Pour the sherry into a small bowl. Take a biscuit and soak it in the sherry for about 10 seconds.

❸ Soak the next biscuit and sandwich it to the previous one with whipped cream. Repeat the procedure until you have a log of cream-sandwiched biscuits on a large serving plate.

❹ Use the remaining cream to cover the log completely. Crumble the flake over the log.

❺ Chill in the refrigerator until ready to serve.

Geoff Skrone
Upavon, Wiltshire

Preparation Time:	15 minutes
Reader's Tip:	This recipe requires very little preparation and is proof that it is perfectly acceptable to construct something delicious from packets of biscuits and chocolate.

BARBARA'S BROWN COFFEE CAKE

300 g/10 oz soft light brown sugar
300 g/10 oz strong white flour
250 g/8 oz butter or margarine
1 teaspoon baking powder
1 teaspoon cinnamon
250 ml/8 fl oz buttermilk
1 teaspoon baking soda
1 egg
1 teaspoon vanilla essence
1 teaspoon instant coffee
50 g/2 oz pecan nuts

❶ Grease a large flat rectangular cake tin, 20 x 30 cm (8 x 12 inches). Preheat the oven to 190°C/375°F/Gas Mark 5.

❷ Put the sugar, flour, butter or margarine, baking powder and cinnamon in a mixing bowl and mix together. Set aside about 325 g/11 oz of this mixture to top the cake.

❸ Add the buttermilk, baking soda, egg, vanilla essence and instant coffee, and mix well. If the mixture curdles, just add a little more flour.

4 Pour the cake mixture into the prepared cake tin, and sprinkle on the reserved topping. Scatter the pecan nuts on top.

5 Bake in the preheated oven for 35–40 minutes.

Elisabeth Wengersky
South Hampstead, London

'Eat this cake with freshly-brewed coffee for best results.'

Preparation Time:	15 minutes
Cooking Time:	35–40 minutes
Oven Temperature:	190°C/375°F/Gas Mark 5
Reader's Tip:	In the absence of buttermilk, you can always use ordinary milk.

LINZER TORTE

200 g/7 oz strong white flour
1 teaspoon baking powder
125 g/4 oz slightly salted
  butter, chilled
125 g/4 oz freshly ground
  fresh hazelnuts or almonds
125 g/4 oz caster sugar
15 g/$\frac{1}{2}$ oz vanilla sugar
2 drops bitter almond oil
1$\frac{1}{2}$ teaspoons ground
  cinnamon

$\frac{1}{4}$ teaspoon ground cloves
1 egg white
$\frac{1}{2}$ egg yolk

Filling
250 g/8 oz tangy-flavoured
  jam, such as raspberry, red-
  currant or morello cherry

Topping
$\frac{1}{2}$ egg yolk
1 teaspoon milk

1 Grease and line a round 26 cm/10$\frac{1}{2}$ inch spring–release cake tin. Preheat the oven to 180°C/350°F/Gas Mark 4.

2 Sieve the flour and baking powder on to a clean work surface, making a large well in the middle.

3 Coarsely grate the chilled butter all over the flour and sprinkle on the ground nuts, then put the caster sugar, vanilla sugar, almond oil, cinnamon, ground cloves, egg white and the half egg yolk into the well.

4 With your hands, work the dough together, first mixing the ingredients in the middle together and then gradually adding the flour. If the dough will not stick together, add a little water to bring it together.

5 When the dough is in one big ball, cut it in half and shape the 2 halves into balls. Put in a bowl or wrap them in cling-film, and chill them in the fridge for at least 30 minutes for the pastry to rest. If your dough is quite soft, pop it in the freezer for 20 minutes so that it hardens up enough to roll out more easily.

6 Roll out one of the balls so that it covers the base only of your greased and lined tin. Line the tin, and go round the edges, pressing upwards a little. If the pastry is too soft and falls apart when you try to line the tin, you can take little bits of the pastry and press them into the tin with the back of a spoon until you have covered the base.

7 Spread the jam onto the base, leaving a 1 cm/$^1/_2$ inch border all around.

8 Roll out the remaining ball of pastry to the same size as the first one, and cut out enough strips to make a lattice pattern on top of the torte. If they are too long, don't worry – you can trim them up.

9 Seal the edges by pressing round the edges with a fork. Mix together the egg yolk and milk, and brush the top with this mixture. Bake in the preheated oven for 25–30 minutes.

Elisabeth Wengersky
South Hampstead, London

Preparation Time:	20 minutes
Cooking Time:	25–30 minutes
Oven Temperature:	180°C/350°F/Gas Mark 4
Reader's Tip:	This is a traditional Austrian tart. The butter needs to be chilled, or even frozen, so that it can be grated easily. It is important not to overcook the tart, so watch it carefully during the cooking process.

Elisabeth's Bottomless Cheesecake

a little butter, for greasing

500 g/1 lb curd cheese or fromage frais

150 ml/¼ pint soured cream

3 medium eggs, separated

grated rind of ½ lemon, plus a few drops lemon juice

50 g/2 oz currants or raisins (optional)

1 teaspoon cornflour or custard powder

½ teaspoon salt

3 heaped tablespoons sugar

15 g/¼ oz vanilla sugar

strawberries or kiwi fruit, sliced, to decorate

❶ Lightly grease a 23 cm/9 inch flan dish using a little butter. Preheat the oven to 120°C/250°F/Gas Mark ½.

❷ Put the curd cheese or fromage frais, soured cream, egg yolks, lemon rind and juice, currants or raisins, cornflour or custard powder, salt and 2 tablespoons of the sugar in a mixing bowl and mix well.

❸ Beat the egg whites and, when they begin to stiffen, gently add the remaining sugar and the vanilla sugar.

❹ Gently fold the egg whites into the cheese mixture using a metal spoon.

❺ Pour into the prepared flan dish and bake in the preheated oven for about 1–1½ hours or until set.

6 Allow to cool and decorate with sliced strawberries or kiwi fruit.

Elisabeth Wengersky
South Hampstead, London

'*This is the very best cheesecake*
I have ever eaten.'

Preparation Time:	20 minutes
Cooking Time:	1–1½ hours
Oven Temperature:	120°C/250°F/Gas Mark ½
Reader's Tip:	Make this in the dish in which you wish to serve it, as it does not transfer easily. It is easy to make your own vanilla sugar. Put a vanilla pod in an airtight jar of caster sugar, and leave until required. The longer you leave it, the stronger the vanilla flavour. If you decide not to use the soured cream, perhaps because you're watching your figure, you should use only 2 eggs.

GINGER BISCUIT CAKE

300 ml/¹/₂ pint double cream
2 or 3 pieces stem ginger,
  finely chopped, plus 2
  tablespoons of the syrup
24 ginger nuts

❶ Whisk the cream until stiff.

❷ Add the stem ginger and syrup.

❸ Sandwich the biscuits together with ginger-flavoured cream and arrange in three columns of eight biscuits each on a large sheet of aluminium foil. Cover the biscuits with the remaining cream, then wrap up in foil and freeze.

❹ Finally, remove from the freezer about 15 minutes before serving.

Lindy Moffatt
Hadlow Down, Sussex

Preparation Time: 10 minutes

Reader's Tip: This cake makes a delicious pudding. An alternative to the use of stem ginger is to flavour the cream with crushed chocolate chip biscuits and coffee. Another idea is to melt some plain chocolate and drizzle this over the assembled cake.

ACKNOWLEDGEMENTS

This book could not have been written without the help of many readers of *The Daily Telegraph*, including:

Muriel Allan, Lindsey Appleby, Rosie Ashe, Nan Ashman, Mrs. N. Ashworth, M. Atkinson, Heather Baker, Sheila Batten, Vera Beba, Daphne Blake, Moira Bourke, Michael Box, Pat Brown, Gloria Cann, Judy Cairns, Mrs. E. Clayton, Helen Cleave, M. Combourcha, Rosemary Cowan, Pam Daniels, Janet Dayer-Smith, Anne Dean, Eileen and Jenny, Sarah Donald, Valerie Dunne, Mary Dyson, Elizabeth, Emma Gardner, Gillian and Yvonne, Pauline Fairweather, Delia Gaze, Mary Gillies, Margaret Green, Jo Haines, Dorothy Harcourt, Jenny Heughan, Christine Hill, Norah Hinde, Griselda Hobson, Tony Hogger, Vera Hopwood, Sue Horsham, Jean Hurley, Sarah Innes, Barbara Jackson, Ivy Jarvis, Helen Kaczmarczuk, Cecilia J. Kee, Mrs. J.T. Kenner, J. K., Betty Jones, Daphne King-Brewster, Liz Kirkwood, Michael Lane, Anne Larpent, Diane Lawton, Joy Macdonald, Angela Master, Ann Meddings, Anne Mocatta, Lindy Moffatt, Mrs. J.V. Moss, Helen Orchard, Phillip D. Pearson, Rachel Perry, E. Ridout, Geoff Skrone, Karin Smith, Rev. Raymond Smith, Barbara Steele, Pamela Stevens, Gwen Stevenson, Patricia J. Stockham, Edna Terry, Susan Tomkins, Miss J.C. Turner, Elisabeth Wengersky, Mrs. M. West, Doreen Williamson, Marion Wilson, Jill M. White, Pam Whitwam and John Wright.

Every effort has been made by the Publishers and *The Daily Telegraph* to contact each individual contributor. If any recipe has appeared without proper acknowledgement, the Publishers and *The Daily Telegraph* apologise unreservedly. Please address any queries to the editor, c/o the Publishers.

INDEX

Three ways to order *Right Way* books:

(1) Visit www.constablerobinson.com and order through our website.

(2) Telephone the TBS order line on 01206 255 800.
Order lines are open Monday – Friday, 8:30am – 5:30pm.

(3) Use this order form and send a cheque made payable to **TBS Ltd** or charge my [ ] Visa [ ] Mastercard [ ] Maestro (issue no)

Card number: _____

Expiry date: _____ Last three digits on back of card: _____

Signature: _____

(your signature is essential when paying by credit or debit card)

No. of copies	Title	Price	Total
	Easy Jams, Chutneys and Preserves	£5.99	
	The Curry Secret	£5.99	
	The New Curry Secret	£7.99	
	For P&P add £2.75 for the first book, 60p for each additional book **Grand Total**		£

Name: _____
Address: _____
_____ Postcode: _____

Daytime Tel. No./Email _____
(in case of query)

Please return forms to Cash Sales/Direct Mail Dept., The Book Service, Colchester Road, Frating Green, Colchester CO7 7DW.

Enquiries to readers@constablerobinson.com.

Constable and Robinson Ltd (directly or via its agents) may mail, email or phone you about promotions or products.

[ ] Tick box if you do not want these from us [ ] or our subsidiaries.

www.constablerobinson.com